Helen Hershawende

How to Get There from Here

To Helen,
Thank you for
having me at the
book group - it was fun -
Michelle Berry
'97

How to Get There from Here

by

Michelle Berry

TURNSTONE PRESS

Turnstone Press
607 – 100 Arthur Street
Winnipeg, Manitoba
R3B 1H3 Canada

Turnstone Press gratefully acknowledges the assistance of the
Canada Council and the Manitoba Arts Council.

Some of these stories have appeared previously. "Directions:
How to Get There from Here" was published in *Perhaps?*,
"A Familiar Tune" in *Enigma: The Magazine*, "Do You Know Who
Emily Carr Is?" and "Driving Lessons" in *Blood & Aphorisms*,
"Velcro and Penguins" in *McGill Street Magazine*, "A Really Good
Joke" in *The Malahat Review*, "Bug Shields and Gun Racks" in *Ink
Magazine*, "The Diner" in *Black Cat 115*, "John and the
One-Armed Woman" in *The New Quarterly*, and "Did You Ever
Hear Such a Tale in Your Life?" in *Prism International*.

Cover artwork: "Masquerade" (acrylic on wood with
relief carving, 1993) by Andrew Valko

Design: Manuela Dias

This book was printed and bound in Canada
by Friesens for Turnstone Press.

Canadian Cataloguing in Publication Data
· Berry, Michelle, 1968—
How to get there from here
ISBN 0-88801-212-8
I. Title
PS8553.E7723H68 1997   C813'.54   C97-920024-5
PR9199.3.B4164H68 1997

This book is for my family:
Dad, Mom, Dave and Abigail
and especially for Stuart

—with much love.

Acknowledgements

For support and encouragement my thanks go to: Connie and Leon Rooke, Janice Kulyk-Keefer, Manuela Dias, Meggan Janes, Danette Cairns, friends at PEN Canada, and to the Ontario Arts Council for a Works-in-Progress grant. Special thanks go to Joe Kertes and David Arnason for their impeccable editing.

Table of Contents

Did You Ever Hear Such a Tale in Your Life? /1

A Really Good Joke /7

Velcro and Penguins /15

Jesus on a Tortilla Shell /23

Driving Lessons /31

Directions: How to Get There from Here /37

The Glass Piano /49

Do You Know Who Emily Carr Is? /57

The Most Peculiar Thing /59

A Familiar Tune /69

Swinging High /77

The Diner /87

Bug Shields and Gun Racks /95

Orange Cowboy Boots /103

Cosmetics /109

John and the One-Armed Woman /117

An Urban Myth /125

The Orange /133

Two Hours North of the City /141

"Begin at the beginning," the King said, very gravely, "and go on till you come to the end; then stop."

—Lewis Carroll,
Alice's Adventures in Wonderland

Did You Ever Hear
Such a Tale in Your Life?

*T*here are two men standing in front of Lisa in the line-up at the grocery store. They are holding hands. Lisa looks down at her hands and feels the weight of the potatoes tugging at her wrists.

"Oh my God," one of the men says. He drops the other's hand.

"What?"

"Potatoes! We forgot to get potatoes!"

They are almost to the front of the line. The one man looks back at the large line-up. He scans the aisles. He puts his hand up over his eyes, as if he's shading them, and scans the aisles for something that will tell him where the potatoes are.

"We'll get them on the way home," his friend tells him. His friend takes his hand again. "Don't worry. We'll get them later. We're almost at the front of the line."

"I could run. I could run for the potatoes and, by the time you're up at the cash, I'd be back." He drops the other's hand again.

Lisa watches.

"No," he says. "No. I couldn't leave you here. I couldn't leave you alone."

He says this so quietly that Lisa is a little afraid she hasn't heard it right. She moves in closer. She pretends to read the *Weekly World News*.

"Baby Alien Hatched from Dinosaur Egg," the front page shouts.

"Woman with Seven Heads Meets Headless Man and Falls in Love."

The two men are holding hands again and the potato worrier looks like he might cry. His friend is looking at his feet. He admires his green Doc Martens and then plays with the red handle of his grocery cart.

Lisa looks around at the cavernous store. She hears the echoes of hundreds of shopping carts' squeaky wheels.

"What about the yams? We can use the yams instead of potatoes," the one man says.

"No. That just won't do."

Lisa is desperately trying not to stare at them. She focuses on the large, black print in front of her.

"Man Caught in Cyclone for Eight Days Eats Own Leg to Stay Alive."

"I still have time to get them. Look. That man is so slow. I could be back in less than a minute."

"Don't leave me alone!" The one man shouts this.

Lisa looks up. The two men are staring hard at each other.

The potato man has blond hair. It is dyed blond and his mustache is red. The effect is startling. The other man is bald. He isn't bald by nature, he's had it done somewhere. Lisa can see the stubble growing back. It is patchy and dark.

Behind Lisa are a woman and a man. They are both shuffling awkwardly from foot to foot. Their small child is sitting in their half-empty grocery cart, singing "Three Blind Mice" and eating Arrowroot cookies.

"Homosexuals," the man hisses at the woman. Lisa stares at him. She doesn't care if he sees her. "Homosexuals," he says again. The man says this with such contempt that Lisa is suddenly afraid.

She moves closer to the two men, picks up the *Weekly World News* and opens it to page one.

Three blind mice.

Three blind mice.

See how they run.

See how they run . . .

Lisa reads the caption under the picture of the woman with seven heads. It reads: "Nice legs, shame about the heads."

"I'm just nervous alone," the bald man says. "I just feel so vulnerable."

"I know, I know." The potato man is caressing the bald man's back. Lisa can hear the man behind her hissing something. He sounds like a snake. Or a gas leak. "I'm sorry. I just wanted potatoes."

The woman at the check-out looks haggard and rushed. She groans when she looks up and sees how long the line is.

"Marianne, open check-out six, please," she calls into the microphone next to her. Half of her line-up rushes to check-out six but when they get there it is closed. Lisa transfers her bag of potatoes from one hand to the other.

All Lisa has is potatoes. She's on this potato diet and all she can eat for six days are potatoes. She can cook them any way she pleases (fry, bake, microwave, roast), she can buy all types (white, red, P.E.I., sweet), she just can't eat anything but potatoes. When she saw Mark on the street with Tina she decided to try the diet.

Mark.

Lisa's ex. The ex-boyfriend who left Lisa because she wasn't ethnic enough, because her past was no nasty secret, because she had no clouded history. She wasn't different. Like the potato man and his lover. Lisa thinks she can't lose anything by trying the potato diet. Anything but weight.

The seven-headed woman looks a lot like Tina. At least she has Tina's body. Small and shapely with large breasts. And one of the heads does bear a mild resemblance—all that kinky black hair and those dark, piercing eyes.

"When we are separated I feel so . . ."

"Vulnerable?"

"No, I said that already. I feel exposed."

"Isn't that the same as vulnerable?"

"I guess so."

The bald man spits on his finger and cleans the toe of his Doc Marten with it.

Lisa hears a hiss from behind.

"Can't you say anything nice?" the woman behind Lisa whispers to the hissing man.

"Faggots," he says.

They all ran after the farmer's wife,
Who cut off their tails with a carving knife.

The two men turn, look at Lisa and then stare at the hissing man. Lisa turns red. She can feel it spread across her face. She feels like she's the one who has hissed. Or she feels like she's just seen Mark with his hand on Tina's hair, smoothing it, pulling down on the kinks and curls. The man behind her whispers something to the woman and then they pull their cart out of line and walk over to check-out six. Lisa sees all these confused people at check-out six just waiting for Marianne to open up.

"Marianne, open check-out six!" Lisa's check-out woman screams this into the microphone. The store suddenly goes quiet. She blushes. "Sorry," she says to the old man trying to pay his bill in pennies. He ignores her and keeps counting.

"A dollar eighty-six, a dollar eighty-seven . . ." His total reads $20.04.

Lisa sighs. Then the two men in front of her start kissing. Their tongues move in and out of each other's mouths.

The *Weekly World News* hasn't told Lisa anything she doesn't already know.

Mark is gone and Lisa might just be better for it.

She can hear faint singing coming from the child at check-out six.

Did you ever hear such a tale in your life?
Three blind mice.

She looks over at check-out six, at the child singing in the grocery cart, and sees the hissing man staring at the two kissing men in front of her. She shivers.

"Here." She moves up close to the kissing men and hands them her bag of potatoes. "Here. You have them. I don't need them."

"God, thank you," they say, in unison.

"How nice of you," says the potato man.

The bald man touches her arm with the finger he spit on and Lisa leaves the line-up and moves quickly out of the store. A breeze from the cars rushing past on the street hits her face. A streetcar screeches menacingly. A man asks her for spare change. Out on the street Lisa realizes she is still carrying the copy of the *Weekly World News*. She opens it and looks again at the seven-headed woman. She looks at the woman's body. Just like Tina's body. There is no picture of the headless man she has fallen in love with but Lisa thinks that he must be handsome to get a woman with a body like that. Then she laughs. She doubles up, laughing on the street, thinking of a handsome headless man and what that could possibly mean.

People stop to look at her. She stops laughing and walks on.

Across the street Lisa sees a blond, pimply woman in a red check-out outfit. She is sitting on a park bench, chewing gum. She is holding her chubby arms around her chest, rocking, in the cold of the day. Lisa crosses over and sits beside her. She leans over, pretending to get something out of her knapsack, and looks at the woman's name tag. "Marianne," it says in large, pink letters.

"Excuse me," Lisa says. Her voice is dry.

"What?"

"You're wanted on check-out six," Lisa says.

Marianne looks at her like she's crazy. "Pardon me?"

"In the store," Lisa says. "Check-out six." She points towards the grocery store.

"Yeah, well, I quit," Marianne says and then she starts to cry.

Lisa hands her the *Weekly World News* she is still holding. Marianne takes it and opens to page one.

5

"Nice body," she says. She is looking at the seven-headed woman. "Too bad about all those heads."

"They could come in handy," Lisa says. She sees the two men, holding hands, walking out of the grocery store. Her potatoes are somewhere in their bag.

"For what?" Marianne stops reading and chewing and crying and looks at Lisa. Her eyes are puffy and a pimple near her upper lip has burst. There is a drop of blood on it.

"You could see behind you, you could talk to yourself and no one would think you were crazy, you could eat seven different flavours of ice cream, you could sing and it would sound like a concert, you could—"

"I get the picture." Marianne doesn't seem impressed. "I'd rather have one head," she says, "even if it is this ugly one." She gets up, takes the *Weekly World News* with her, and walks, shoulders stooped, towards the grocery store.

The bald man and the potato man wave at Lisa from across the street. She waves back. They walk away, hand in hand.

Lisa sits there, on the cold, green park bench, thinking about things.

A Really Good Joke

"*H*e thinks he is God," she says. "God or Jesus, I can't tell which."

Davis nods.

"You ate our babies!" the man shouts.

The police sirens stop. Davis' partner, Joe, is standing back by the cruiser and he has just now turned the sirens off.

"You ate our babies!"

They are standing in someone's back yard. It is night.

"I am God," the man shouts. "You ate our babies."

It is late and they are standing in the back yard of someone's house. In the yard are vegetables in stages of half-decay. There are also weeds creeping up the wire fences. They are standing there, in the dark, surrounded by rotting vegetables and creeping weeds, watching a man who thinks he is God.

"Do you think he's on drugs?" Davis asks.

She looks at him as if he is crazy. "What do you think?" She laughs. "You think he really is God?" She laughs again. Her laughter rings out into the back yard, bumps up against the wire fences and stops.

It is strangely silent in the dark yard. Silent except for the screaming man. Davis looks up into the windows of the house and sees that the curtains are bed sheets. From a split in the bed-sheet curtain of a room on the third floor of the house a small face peers out at him. Davis waves at the small, dark face pushed up to the glass in the third-floor window. He waves and then he notices that the sheet happens to be a Peter Puck sheet, one of his favourites when he was young.

"Take your baton out," she says, disturbing his train of thought. He looks at her. Her face is squinched up in concentration. "He could be dangerous."

"All-powerful," Davis says. He smiles. "He'll knock our batons out of our hands with a breath of air."

She laughs. "Now you're getting the hang of it."

Davis doesn't know her name but he's heard she's a good cop. He's heard that she's only been out of the academy for three years and she's already up there with the best.

Davis looks around and sees Joe standing by the side door of the cruiser. He's got his shoulders up in a shrug and his long legs crossed out in front of him. He's sharing a coffee with the other cop and they are listening to the radio.

"I'm Siren." Her voice comes out of the darkness, right close to his shoulder.

"Pardon?" he says.

"My name, it's Siren." She waits. She tenses. Davis can tell she's waiting for the jokes. She is waiting for the billion jokes that are sitting on the tip of Davis' tongue.

"I'm Davis," he says.

"Pleased to meet you." She moves her baton to her left side and shakes his outstretched hand.

"Siren, eh?"

"Yeah."

They are silent.

"You ate our babies!" the man shouts. "You ate our babies!"

Davis looks back at Joe and Siren's partner, leaning on the police cruiser. Movement has been stalled because the radio dispatcher can't get a fix on who the man is. They have to get a fix on him or they can't move forward. They have to know what he is carrying, what weapon he is packing, they have to know if he is wanted. The dispatcher is checking the records right now for escaped criminals in the area, or drug dealers or wife-beaters. Davis looks up at the windows again. The Peter Puck face has been forcefully pulled back into the room by an adult and now Davis is looking at a soft, fuzzy, slept-on head of hair. The head opens the window.

"What's going on down there?" she calls into the silence.

Siren jumps a little, Davis feels the movement through the soles of his boots.

"Close your window, ma'am," he shouts. "We've got a situation developing down here."

"A criminal?" the woman shouts. "Is he dangerous?"

Davis shrugs.

The woman closes her window rapidly and then the child's face pops up to look out and the woman pulls him back.

"Hey, Joe," Davis calls. "You should knock on the door out front and tell them what's going on."

"After I finish my coffee," Joe says.

Davis sighs.

"Lazy, eh?" Siren chuckles.

"You ate our babies!" the man cries.

Siren's partner comes up to them. He walks carefully around the vegetables and then he taps his boots on the fence, first one, then the other, to get the dirt out. "What's up?" he asks.

"Davis, Reg," Siren says. "Second Division."

The two men shake hands.

"Hey, I hear you got a new water cooler down there," Reg says. He looks impressed. "Man, we don't even have a coffee machine that works. I gotta bring my own." Reg points his thumb back at Joe who is filling up his coffee from Reg's dark green thermos.

Davis looks at Reg's face in the dark. He peers at it. He can't help himself. There is a scar on Reg's face that looks as if a shark bit him.

9

"Knife fight," Reg says. He moves under the light from the moon and turns his face up for Davis' benefit. "Situation kind of like this," he says.

Davis nods. He appreciates a good scar the way a painter appreciates form.

"Dispatcher got back to you yet?" Siren asks.

"Nope."

"Why don't we just ask him his name?" Davis asks. That's what he would have done in the first place. That's what he would have done if Eighth Division hadn't shown up at exactly the same time. If Joe had just sped up slightly and cut the man off at the corner, as Davis had asked him to, then Eighth Division wouldn't even have crossed their paths and Joe and Davis would have been back in the car by now, sharing a joke about this man who thinks he is God.

"Could be carrying," Siren says.

"Yeah," says Reg.

Davis thinks about this. "Wouldn't he have shot us by now if he was carrying?"

The three police officers quickly look away from one another. Davis knows it's a breach of protocol to question another cop but he is getting frustrated just standing there.

"Well?" Davis tries again. "What do you think?"

"You ate our babies!"

The man isn't wearing a shirt and for the first time Davis notices he has no shoes on either. He has his arms up in the air and he's shouting "You ate our babies" with all his might.

"Hey, you!" Davis moves his baton back and forth in his hands so the man can see he's carrying protection. "Hey, what's your name?"

The man staggers around and looks straight at Davis. He holds his arms out, indicating the sky. "I'm God," he says.

Davis shivers. He moves towards the man.

Joe walks up to Reg and Siren. "Dispatcher says his name is probably Friendly. It's a gang name," he says to them. "Says that, if it's the right guy, he's on drugs most likely and he isn't registered to a weapon."

"That don't mean anything," Reg says. He points to his scar.

Joe nods.

Siren moves up towards Davis, who is about twenty feet away from the man and whacking his baton into the palm of one hand.

"So, God," Davis is saying. He chuckles to himself because a million jokes are coming right at him. Jokes about a lady cop named Siren and a man who thinks he is God.

"You ate my baby," the man says quietly. He dances in a strange pattern across the rotting vegetables. His feet move, one two three four, across the dirt, stamping prints into the soil.

"Hey, man," Davis says. "What's your real name? Tell me your real name. I won't hurt you." His voice is kind and soft. He pretends he's talking to the little boy in the window with the Peter Puck sheet-curtains.

Suddenly, the man lunges and Davis snaps his baton back across the man's shoulders. He hears a crack.

"Shit!" Davis screams.

The man rushes back, away from Davis, and starts pulling viciously at the weeds along the fence.

"You OK?" Siren asks. She twirls her baton around her back like a majorette and then pats Davis on the shoulder with it.

"Caught me off guard," Davis says. He can hear Joe laughing in the background.

"His name's Friendly," Siren says.

"Oh Christ," Davis says. He scratches his head. "Siren, Friendly and God! Man!" He shakes his head and chuckles.

Siren looks at Davis and then she walks closer to the man clutching at the fence. "Hey, Friendly," she says. "Hey there, Friendly."

The man pulls at the weeds and cries, "I am God, I am God, I am God," over and over.

Davis looks up at the house and sees the little boy and the woman silhouetted against the Peter Puck sheet. The woman is stroking the little boy's hair.

Siren makes her way slowly to the man. Joe and Reg stand

back, their hands on their guns. Davis thinks that it is almost as if they are testing her. He thinks about how, if she were just about anyone else on the force, they would be there with her, approaching the man in a line. And then he thinks about how Siren herself seems to be in on this. She is confidently moving towards the man who thinks he is God and she is not asking for backup. She is doing this on her own, daring fate, showing off, proving something.

Davis shakes his head. He watches Siren for a moment longer and then he moves quickly to join her. When he does so the man who thinks he is God turns quickly back and kicks high with his bare foot. It catches Siren's face and knocks her to the ground. Friendly jumps on her and begins to punch her face and head. He punches her all over her head and neck and face. She doesn't put her hands up to block the punches, but lies there and takes them.

Davis runs up and pulls Friendly off Siren. Joe and Reg rush up. Siren lies there, dazed, blood coming out of one nostril.

"You OK?" Reg asks.

"Yeah, fine." Siren pulls herself up. She wipes her nose with the back of her hand. "He's not too friendly, is he?" She laughs and then Reg and Joe laugh too. Joe punches her on the shoulder in a friendly way and then they all turn toward Davis and the man.

"You ate our babies," the man is saying to Davis, who has him pinned to a fence. The man's body is pinned up against the fence and Davis is trying to pry his fingers off the wire. The man is talking to Davis as if they are old friends. His voice is calm. He says "You ate our babies, you ate our babies, you ate our babies" very calmly as Davis pries at his fingers. Each time one finger is removed another one clutches at the fence.

Joe and Reg and Siren watch.

Siren wipes the flow of blood from her nose with her sleeve.

Davis pries helplessly at the fingers.

"You ate our babies," the man says.

The little boy on the third floor of the house suddenly opens his window and shouts out into the silent night air.

"Pigs!" He shouts it so loud that all four officers look up toward the house, toward the boy and his Peter Puck curtains. Davis' grasp loosens and the man who thinks he is God uses this distraction to make a dash for it, out into the street. He rushes, full swing, into the street and into an oncoming car. His bungling body, his crude gait cease abruptly when the large car smacks into him and sends him rolling toward the curb.

Joe, Davis, Reg and Siren watch him roll and then stop rolling and lie there like a bag of potatoes.

The boy in the window shouts "Pigs!" again, so loud that it hurts Davis' ears.

The woman driving the car gets out quickly and rushes toward the man. Her shrill scream slowly takes the form of words and Davis finally hears her shouting "Oh my God, oh my God, oh my God," over and over.

Davis radios an ambulance while Siren, Joe and Reg cover the man with sheets from the back of the woman's car.

The frizzy-haired woman comes out of her house. She walks up to Davis, her hands on her hips. "Good way to catch a dangerous criminal." Then she walks back into her house and turns off all the lights. Davis can't see the little boy anymore. The Peter Puck sheets look like plain curtains in the darkness.

Siren, Reg, Joe and Davis surround the sheeted body of the man and listen to the screaming of the woman with the car.

"Oh my God," she screams. "Oh my God, oh my God!"

The distant howl of the ambulance gradually draws nearer through the night. And, as the sounds move in and out of his ears, as he scratches his head and watches the motionless, sheet-draped body, Davis thinks about how all of this, this whole night, this entire fiasco, will make a really good joke. He thinks about how funny the whole thing will be tomorrow down at the station, the guys laughing their heads off by the brand new water cooler. He shakes his head and thinks about how he will start the joke. He'll start it with, "There's a drugged guy named Friendly and a police lady named Siren standing in the back yard of this house . . ." Something like that. Then he'll tell them all about the Peter Puck curtains and the boy screaming "Pigs!"

The ambulance pulls up beside Friendly's body and Davis watches the attendants check for a heartbeat. He watches them and thinks about an ending for the joke.

"Oh my God, oh my God," the woman screams when the attendants pull the sheet over Friendly's face.

Davis shakes his head and scratches his chin, the ambulance drives off, Joe pours himself another cup from Reg's thermos, Siren yawns loudly, and the woman with the car lies down on the ground and cries. He stands there, in the dark, thinking hard about an ending that would be funny and draws a blank—absolutely nothing funny comes to mind.

Velcro and Penguins

We are on the beach. Actually, I am on the beach and he is walking down the ramp towards the beach and towards me. I am lying on a large beach blanket. I am spread out as seductively as I can manage. This is not easy. It's not easy because my mother made me take the beach blanket that has penguins on it and I am attempting both to be sexy and, at the same time, to cover up the penguins with my legs and arms. I am wearing a Walkman and listening to the radio. It is the last day of my summer vacation. I am listening to a talk show on CBC-AM. This isn't something I'd normally be doing but it gives me lots to think about while I lie here on the beach and watch him come down the ramp and walk towards me.

Here he comes.

The talk show is about mothers and daughters. Actually, it's about daughters who have recently lost their mothers. Lost them as in death, not as in losing them at the shopping mall or something. The show is really about how tough the mother-daughter relationship is. It's like friction. It's like, when the mother likes the daughter, the daughter hates the mother. You know. Like that. Friction. Or like Velcro. It's like Velcro, ripping and sticking.

The Velcro on my beach wrap has stopped sticking because there is fuzz and sand in the sticky part. I stopped bringing it to the beach with me last week.

He is coming right over towards me. I cover several penguins with my bum and then I spread my hair in a fan across a penguin wearing Bermuda shorts. I lie perfectly still so as not to scare him away.

All morning I've been lying here, listening to this program and waiting for him to walk towards me. The sun has gone behind the clouds and come back out and gone back in. I've listened to first-person accounts of over fifteen deaths. Fifteen mothers leaving fifteen daughters. Fifteen daughters losing fifteen mothers.

That's not actually true. Sometimes sisters called in together and then it was only one mother for two daughters.

"Hi," he says.

My mouth is open. I'm not sure he's really said it. I sit up on my blanket and I look up at him. I take off my headphones and stare at him.

"Hi," he says again.

This time I'm sure he said it and I smile up at him like he's God or something.

I lie back down, put my headphones back on and turn the volume down low.

He fluffs out his beach towel, solid purple, and carefully stretches it out, just to the left of me, over flat sand. He reaches into his knapsack and pulls out suntan lotion (two bottles), a magazine, glasses (he wears glasses?) and an apple. He arranges all this around him. He's very tidy. Then he takes off his shirt and it's a good thing I'm lying down because I could have fainted. I mean, I've been looking at his chest from a distance all summer now but up close it's almost twice as large and muscular. That chest makes up for anything he's missing in his face. It makes up for the beaky nose and the hairless eyebrows. All I can think about is what Rita would say if she could see me now.

"Come here often?" he asks and I think, *that's a stupid line*, but I answer anyway with a nod and a small smile. I turn the volume back up, but leave it at the level where I can hear him and the show at the same time.

That line is something I've heard a billion times on TV even if no one has actually ever said it to me before. It's one of those things you just think no one really says. It's almost like an urban myth, it's out there somewhere, floating in the distance, but it hasn't really happened to anyone you know.

He is smearing his chest with oily lotion so I forgive him for the line. Then he uses another type of lotion for his face. It's less oily.

"My mother died two months ago," a tearful voice says in my ear. The voice is coming in my left ear, the announcer in my right. Something's wrong with my Walkman. I smack it and shake it and fiddle with the headphone plug but their voices are still staying separate in my ears. He is too busy touching himself to notice my jerky movements.

"My mother and I were very close," she says. "Her death was so unexpected."

The announcer says something about the fact that any death is unexpected, even long, lingering ones, and I nod to myself because when my grandpa died I knew he was dying but the whole thing knocked me out anyway.

All of a sudden I look up at him and I realize he's been talking to me.

"Pardon me?"

"I said that you should turn over or you're going to burn your stomach," he says. His voice is nasally, nothing I really expected. I expected smooth, deep, syrupy. But it's nasally and, now that I really look, his complexion is pretty bad too. That's why he uses two types of suntan lotion. Suddenly I realize that I've been waiting all summer to meet this guy just because of his chest and then he gets up close and he grosses me out. Typical. Just like most things in life. Like TV. From a distance TV is great, but when you get up close to it it's all drugs and diseases and fake, costumed people.

I turn over onto my stomach. I can feel him checking out my bum. Or, maybe he's looking at the penguins.

"I fought with her just before she died," the woman says. "We were discussing clothing, something I'd worn that she thought didn't become me." The woman laughs, slightly. "And then we argued and I told her to mind her own business." I'm nodding because the whole thing sounds so familiar. "I told her to let me live my own life for once and then"—the voice chokes up—"she had a heart attack. Right there. While I was on the phone with her."

"Oh God," I say.

"What?" he asks. "Did you say something?" He is lying back on his purple beach towel reading his magazine. It's a *GQ* magazine. He is checking out the fall fashions. For some reason that makes me laugh. It's something Rita would go for but I prefer guys who read *The New Yorker* even if they only do it for the cartoons. Actually, I've never in my life met a guy who reads *The New Yorker*, but if I ever did I'm sure that's the guy I'd go for.

"I'm listening to the radio," I say. I point towards the Walkman just in case there is nothing between his ears.

"Oh," he says. "Anything interesting?"

"Guilt is a major factor when anyone close to you dies," the announcer says. "People often dredge up old arguments, old disputes, things they shouldn't have said or . . ."

"Anything worth listening to?" he shouts. He points towards the Walkman in my hand.

"Yes."

"Well, what?"

He is really starting to eat at me. Here I've been waiting an entire summer to meet him. I've seen him at the store, on the beach, at the campsite, around Dell's Pool Hall. I've been checking out his developing tan, his developing chest. I've forgiven his nose and his eyebrows. But then, he gets up close, and he says stupid things like "You come here often?" and interrupts me when I'm busy with something and for some reason I suddenly feel like spitting at him.

"God," the woman is sobbing. "If I'd only just been nicer to her . . ."

"Don't blame yourself," the announcer says. "You have to get away from the blaming stage."

I turn my body until I'm lying, once again, on my back. I look up at the sky.

"It's a talk show," I say. My anger has scared me a little. I concentrate on his chest. He concentrates on his chest. He rubs his ribs.

"About what?"

I have to hand it to him, he is persistent.

"About Kurt Cobain," I say. "It's about how his lyrics pointed straight to his suicide."

"Really?"

I nod. I like making things up. I get a charge out of it.

"Yeah. You know that song where he sings that he doesn't have a gun? Well, it's really a call for help, a call for attention."

"Yeah, you're right. That makes sense."

"Even the title of that song, 'Smells Like Teen Spirit,' means something. It means . . ." I have to think fast. "It means that, well, you know how the spirit of youth is in guns, right? So the song means that he could smell his death in the blast from the gun." I shake my head. I've gone way too far.

"That's deep," he says. I let out my breath. He looks impressed. "What about his wife?"

"What about her?"

"Or his mother?"

I shrug. I have no idea what he's talking about.

"Didn't they know that his songs were a cry for help? I mean, it seems pretty obvious now. And, besides, I've heard that his wife knew all about his problems."

I think fast. "His mother never listened to his music," I say. "She was very religious and his stuff offended her. I mean, if she'd listened she would have been the only one who could help him. His wife didn't count in his life the way his mother did."

He turns and looks straight at me. "That's not true," he says. "You're making this stuff up."

"What? No, I'm not. Here, listen." I start to hand him my Walkman but then I say, "Oh, shit, the program's over. Now it's something about mothers and daughters."

He just looks at me. He doesn't hold out his hand to take my Walkman or anything. His chest kind of looks shrunken. I can't help but think that Rita would just about fall in love with him right now. She tends to fall for guys who obviously need help.

A man has called in to the radio show. "It's not fair," he says. "I lost my mother too but just because I'm not a woman it's not as hard for me? Is that what you're saying?"

"No, of course not," the announcer says. "It's just that daughters have a certain bond with their mothers, like sons do with fathers, and this bond is what we are exploring today."

He is still looking at me.

"I'm sorry," I say, but then I take it back. "I'm sorry if you don't believe me but what can I do to prove it to you? The show is already over."

He lies back down on his purple towel and he puts his T-shirt over his face. I like him better this way. I feel bad about lying to him—actually, I feel bad about getting caught lying to him—but he was being such a jerk and he's been such a disappointment.

"Summer's almost over," I say. I'm trying to be nice.

He doesn't answer. He just lies there on that damn purple towel with his shirt over his face and soaks in the sun on his muscly chest. I can't help but think that if he let the sun on his face it would dry up his pimples.

The CBC announcer is trying to calm down the man on the radio. The man thinks it isn't fair to suggest that daughters have closer relationships with their mothers. He is practically crying. The announcer keeps saying, "*Different* relationships, not necessarily *closer* relationships." I'm getting tired of the whole show. The whole thing has done nothing but depress me anyway. It's made me think of my mother, up at the campsite, packing all our summer stuff away. It's made me feel bad for taking off to the beach today. It's made me almost think of going up there and helping her.

"So maybe I did make it up," I say. I don't know what makes me say that. Maybe I say that because I want to get something out of my summer here on the beach. I want to have something to take home with me, something to think about. "Why?" He sits up and takes the T-shirt off his face. I swear it's almost like he's been sulking or something. What a baby. Rita would love this.

"Because I was listening to something that I didn't think you'd find interesting." As soon as that comes out of my mouth I know I've said the wrong thing. Now he thinks I like him or something. Him and his damn chest.

He smiles at me. "Oh?" Then he leans over on one elbow and flexes his stupid stomach muscles right at me. I think I might be sick. For some reason my admission that I lied to impress him turns every knob on his body. He becomes unbearably friendly. He starts talking about himself, about his workout schedule and what he eats for dinner, and he just won't stop.

"Tracy." I hear someone calling out for me. I can hear the high-pitched call over top of the CBC announcer and over top of his nasally voice. It's my mother. She is standing up, on top of the ramp, waving both of her arms in the air. "Tracy, honey." She's got some sort of handkerchief on her head to block the sun and she's waving her skinny arms back and forth and up and down.

He is talking away about himself in this nasally voice, my mother is screaming for me and the man on the CBC is shouting at the announcer in my left ear. I look down at the penguins surrounding me and I sigh.

Summer is over. I think about the woman who killed her mother by yelling at her on the telephone. I shake my head. I can't get over that. One minute she's there, screaming at you and you're screaming at her, the next minute she's gone.

Life.

It's like that sometimes.

I stand up and shake out my towel. He's still talking to me but I'm not listening. I'm not listening to anything really. I'm just shaking out my towel and gathering up my stuff and heading up the ramp towards my mom. I want to ask her if she can help me fix the Velcro on my beach wrap for next summer. I want to ask her if she can make it all stick again. I want to ask her if we can actually replace the Velcro, not just clean it out. Get a new piece, something fuzz-free. I wave at her and she uses both arms to wave at me. That handkerchief on her head flaps in the breeze and, as I walk up the ramp towards my mom, I shake out my penguin towel and wrap it carefully around my sunburnt stomach.

Jesus on a Tortilla Shell

*I'*m sitting in front of the TV trying to see the face of Jesus in a tortilla shell when there's a knock on the door.

I ignore it and focus my attention on the tortilla.

I can see his hair in the burned mark, flowing down the side of the tortilla, but I'm having trouble identifying the face. There's a lump somewhere near where his nose should be, but to me it looks like a drop of grease.

Whoever is at the door keeps on knocking.

I turn the volume up on the TV so I can hear what Donahue is saying. He says that over 1,000 people a day visit this tortilla in New Mexico.

Over 1,000 pilgrims going on a tortilla pilgrimage.

The knocking at my door won't stop and all of a sudden I hear someone with a weak little voice calling out, "Anyone home?"

Go away, I think.

The woman who fried this mysterious, spiritual tortilla is sitting on a chair on the stage with her daughter. They are holding hands. The screen cuts in half and now I can see both the woman and her daughter and the tortilla shell. All three of them right there in front of me. I'm starting to make out his chin. It's over by the grease lump, under the cascade of unruly burned hair. The image wavers back and forth in my mind. Sometimes I see it, sometimes I don't.

"Is there anyone home?" says the voice from behind the front door.

I blow my nose in a Kleenex and throw it on the floor with the others. There is a pile of Kleenexes on the floor. A large pile. It is equal to about four boxes.

Donahue is playing the sceptic.

"Jesus on a tortilla shell?" he asks. He lifts his shoulders up and shrugs as if he's not too impressed. "I don't mean to be disrespectful, ma'am," he says, "it's just . . ." He pauses and then he shrugs his shoulders even higher and looks straight at the audience. He delivers the next line with gusto. He separates each word for full effect. "It's just—Jesus on a tortilla shell?"

He laughs out loud.

I laugh out loud.

"I can hear you in there," the voice says and I look around. I look right at the front door. I look right at where the voice is coming from. "Open up. I know you're in there."

"Go away." I growl deeply. I'm trying to sound like a man. I'm trying to scare the voice into leaving. I hear silence.

One thousand people a day coming into your house, I think.

That's incredible.

Donahue's camera crew are now in New Mexico. They have gone down to show us this. They are showing it to us live. There they are in the room with the tortilla. I can see all the people milling about. Some are praying, some just standing there. The tortilla is encased in a black frame. It's between glass. It's on an altar.

"You made an altar for the tortilla?" Donahue asks. The audience laughs.

The mother and daughter nod. The daughter says that a man they didn't even know donated money for the framing and the altar. She stands up to thank him on commercial television. "Why won't you answer the door?" the voice calls out. I jump a little. I had forgotten about the door knocker. "It's freezing out here."

"Go away," I say again. My voice is husky because I haven't talked to anyone for quite awhile. I sound good and mean and male.

Donahue stops questioning the women to introduce the other people on the stage.

This has only just begun, I think.

This is one good episode.

There's a man up on Donahue's stage holding a little white statue of the Virgin Mary. He is stroking her rock-hard hair.

"And you really saw her cry?" Donahue asks.

"Real tears," the man says. "They were salty to taste."

Donahue shrugs.

"Let me in for a minute. Just a minute." The door knocker knocks hard.

"What do you want?" I shout. Even though the front door is directly in front of me I shout to let the voice know how mean I can be.

"I need to show you something," it says. It's a little voice. A little, weak voice. Whoever it is knocks again. Two times. Rap, rap. Just like that.

I want to watch this program. I want to see what will happen next. I wait for Donahue to cut to a commercial break and then I go to the door and open it. I hold my bathrobe around me tightly. I'm about to yell at that little voice.

Outside, standing beside my snow-covered lawn chair, right over by the stack of wet firewood, is a tiny little man with a blue face. I gasp. I rub my eyes. I look again and then I realize that the tiny man is blue because he is cold. His lips are white and raw looking. He is stamping about in the snow and shaking his head back and forth.

"Finally!" he says when he sees me at the door. "Finally!" Then he rushes up and pushes past me into my house.

"Brr," he says. "Close that door."

I'm far too astonished to say much so I close the door and then turn to stare at him. I think I'd be scared if he wasn't so short. A blue man as tiny as he is, pushing his way, uninvited, into my house, isn't all that frightening.

The little blue man is taking off his coat and mittens and scarf. I watch as he throws everything on the staircase.

"Finally," he says again and then he holds out his hand. "Piper O'Bailey," he says. "Pleased to make your acquaintance."

I can hear Donahue in the background. The audience is laughing at something he has said. I'm itching to get back to the set.

"Listen here," I begin. I watch his tiny body stiffen when he hears my tone of voice. He takes a step back, towards the staircase, and opens his mouth wide. "I don't like being disturbed like this," I begin. "I'm not well," I say, "I've been very sick. I'm waiting for the doctor's final results, you see, I'm—" But then he holds up his tiny hand as if he is a traffic cop. He stops my thoughts dead in their track.

I glance at the TV. A bald man is demonstrating how just about anybody can make a statue cry fake tears. He's even got a fake Mona Lisa up on stage with him and she is bawling her eyes out. There are salt streaks running down her chest.

"She can cry for up to two weeks," I can hear him tell Donahue. The audience gasps.

"I haven't got time for this," I begin again in that same tone of voice. "I'm waiting for the doctor to call. I'm supposed to be lying down. I'm not supposed to get up for anything. I'm really very ill." I cough for effect.

The little man hushes me. He actually says "Hush, hush, hush," and then he waves his little finger in front of my eyes.

He has suddenly made me very angry.

"Out!" I command. I'm spitting fire with my eyes. "Don't you see I'm sick?" I point at my bathrobe, my slippers, my pile of Kleenexes, the telephone. "Get out!"

Now the first man on TV, the one with the statue of the Virgin Mary, is telling the audience how the local priest just walked into his house and the statue began to cry. The priest

didn't even touch the statue. "Can you do that?" he challenges
the bald man. "Can you make her cry without touching her?"
The mother and daughter who have the tortilla shell both
gasp. The audience gasps too.

Even though I've threatened him, the little man in my
house doesn't move towards the front door. Instead, he starts to
speak. He speaks quickly and nervously. He uses his hands until
I feel dizzy. He has come about a vacuum, he says. He has come
for the demonstration. His hands rapidly point towards the case
I didn't notice him carrying. I've invited him, he says. He called
last week. I have to listen according to law, he says. I signed
something at Whirr World in the mall. Two weeks ago, when I
was buying an extension cord there, I won this free demonstration with an option to buy. Don't I remember, he says.

Two weeks ago, I think, and then it hits me that two weeks
ago I was healthy as a horse. I was traipsing around malls, buying things, doing things, going to work. I put my hand on my
head to hold back the ache. I rub my temples. I look at the telephone. I sigh.

The little man's hands are everywhere, signalling this and
that. He talks and talks about the vacuum, about its amazing
sucking power, its virtual silence, its self-cleaning-self-fixing-
self-bag-changing-self-storing capabilities. He talks about the
thirty-odd colours it comes in, anything from maroonish blue
to pea-greenish yellow. You can even get black, he says. For the
modern look.

As the little man talks, he unpacks the vacuum. It comes
out of the case neatly and he slides it straight up to a plug. He
is about to unplug the TV when he notices the program. He
stops talking and watches.

Donahue has introduced a woman who videotaped Jesus
and Mary on the curtains in her bedroom.

"He felt this presence," she says of her husband who was
watching a football game in bed at the time. "He felt this presence in the room and he looked around and said to himself,
'There's no one here but me.' That's exactly what he said. The
kids were in the living room. I was doing the dishes. That's

when I heard him screaming and screaming. 'Holy Mother of God,' he screamed. That's exactly what he screamed. Over and over." The woman stops talking, overcome by the moment.

I look at the little man with the vacuum cleaner and he looks at me.

We look back at the TV.

"So you grabbed your video camera . . . ?" Donahue encourages his guest to continue talking.

"Yes," she says. "When I heard him screaming I grabbed the camera and went into the bedroom. That's when I saw it, there on the curtain." The woman points towards the side wall of the studio. Donahue and half the audience look in that direction. The little man in my house looks that way too. I can see his eyes move.

"Just last week my camera crew visited Rosie's home," Donahue says. "And we videotaped this miraculous event for you to see. Take a look." Donahue points the audience towards some far-off direction.

There it is. It's only a reflection of light but it does kind of look like the holy duo. Jesus is large and he is standing in front of Mary who is kneeling at his feet. I can't help but snort.

The little man looks at me. Straight at me.

"Are you laughing at this?" he asks.

"Of course," I say. "It's only a reflection of light."

The little man looks back at the TV set.

"They had a woman on earlier who thought she had burned Jesus' face on a tortilla shell." I start to chuckle. I start to laugh. I start to laugh and then I can't stop. I'm laughing so hard I'm crying. I'm crying and laughing at the same time. I can't breathe. The little man stands there, holding the plug for his vacuum cleaner, and stares at me. I'm laughing so hard I have to sit down to keep from falling. "On a tortilla shell," I manage to gasp out. "Imagine!" I laugh for a long time and whenever I look at the stone-like, still-blue face of the little man in my house I laugh even harder. I feel my sides aching and I feel like I'm going to bust right through my lungs.

The little man just stares at me, that plug in his hand.

Donahue is nodding his head and looking intently at the people on stage.

"Crazy?" he asks. "Are these people crazy?" He pauses. "Are they looking for something that isn't there? Are they looking for something they want to see?"

I nod at Donahue. "Yes, sir," I say and then I giggle and cry a little more. I wipe my eyes with the sleeve of my bathrobe.

"Well, stay tuned for the answers to these questions and much more after a word from our sponsors." Donahue points a long finger straight at me.

I lean back on the couch and look at the little man. He pulls out the plug from the TV and plugs in his vacuum. He moves quietly through the living room and dining room, dragging his mother-of-pearl-silent-as-a-cloud vacuum behind him. He does my sofa and chairs and even pulls at the curtains. He sucks up my pile of Kleenexes. The sucking motion billows the curtains and I can see that it is still snowing outside. The living room is dark and dingy with the TV off. When the little man finishes the downstairs, he pulls the vacuum back towards me and then turns it off. Then he unplugs it and plugs the TV back in. The room glows again.

"Aren't you doing the upstairs too?" I ask.

"You only signed up for the downstairs," he says.

He puts the vacuum back in its case, closes the latch and then stands it up by the front door.

"Well, thank you," I say and then I chuckle a little bit. I'm feeling uncomfortable so I can't help but laugh.

The tiny man pulls himself up until he is about my height and then he sucks in his breath. He looks like he is going to explode. He holds out his hand again when I start to say something. I lean forward on the couch and wait.

Slowly his breath comes out and then, in a raspy, heavily enunciated voice, he says, "Once, a long time ago, I sucked up Jesus in a pale blue vacuum cleaner." He looks straight at me, with his hand up like that, and says this as if he is at confession.

I nod.

I don't know what else to do.

The little man gathers up his coat, his mittens, his scarf and his vacuum cleaner case and rushes quickly out the front door into the whirling snow.

I sit in front of the TV and watch Donahue sum up his program. He talks about the motivation behind seeing things that aren't really there. He talks about what human beings get out of this, why we so desperately need to understand the mysteries of the world, and how we can get in deep trouble by believing the wrong things. He talks about all of this right in front of the mother and daughter who own the spiritual tortilla, right in front of the man and his crying statue, and right in front of the woman with the videotape of the holy reflection.

As the credits roll up the screen I sit on the couch with my feet on the coffee table and glance around at my clean house. I can't even see one clump of cat fur. All my Kleenexes are gone. Amazing, I think. Absolutely amazing. After all that laughing my throat aches and my lungs feel like they've seized up but the ache in my head is gone. I rub my rib cage with my cold hands. I smile.

Then I think about Jesus being sucked into a pale blue vacuum cleaner. I laugh, but not very hard.

Why not? I think.

Why couldn't he be sucked up?

The telephone rings.

Stranger things have happened, I think.

Driving Lessons

We are parked in the driveway, practising. Joe steps on the gas pedal and cranks the wheel around. He makes noises using his lips and tongue.

"Brrummm, brrrummm," he says.

"Always rest your left foot on the clutch," I say. "Joe, listen."

"Brruummmm."

Joe cranks the wheel to the right and smiles at me. He kisses my neck and then makes those noises on my collarbone. His spit leaves a cool mark. I don't want to giggle but I can't help it. It tickles.

Joe turns back to the front of the car and plays with the stickshift. He is pretending he is in a race car. I can tell just from the way he is sitting.

I'll let him play for awhile and then I'll teach him how to drive.

I roll down my window so I can see clearly. I watch my father balancing on the ladder at the front of the house, cleaning the eavestroughs. He cleans them every Saturday unless it's snowing. Sometimes I think that's why my mother moved out.

Joe pokes his finger in my ear.

"Don't," I say. I shake him off like a mosquito. He looks insulted.

"Are you ready yet?"

"Yep." Joe's face takes on the look of concentration I've been waiting for.

"Put your left foot on the clutch, put your right foot on the brake, make sure the car's in neutral and—"

"Do the hokey-pokey and spin yourself around," Joe sings. "That's what it's all about!"

I cross my arms on my chest. "Suit yourself," I say. "We can sit here all day or I can teach you how to drive."

"Sorry," Joe says but he doesn't look sorry at all. He's got this smirk on his face that he can't wash off. His lips are twitching, like he's trying to control it, but that smirk stays on and I feel like punching him.

So I do.

"Ouch." Joe rubs his arm.

"Let's try that again."

Joe puts his feet in the right places but forgets to check if the car's in neutral. It's not and so, when he starts it, we jerk forward and then stall.

"Shit."

My father watches from the highest peak on the roof. He waves and then puts his thumb up.

"Nice work," I say because I know that is what my father would say and that is what drives Joe crazy. He glares at me.

"Finished playing?" I say.

"Jesus, Emily, lighten up will you? You're starting to sound old or something."

Joe is right. Since I've had my licence I've felt older somehow, more responsible. It's like I walked into the Drivers' Testing building a kid and left it an adult. I grew up after several parallel parks and attempting a merge on the highway.

Driving.

It's taken something out of me.

I shrug but Joe misses it as he puts the car in neutral, places his feet on the brake and clutch, pulls up on the emergency brake, and starts the car.

"Not bad," he says. He makes that "brrrum" noise a couple more times and then he looks at me for encouragement. "What next?"

I look at my father on the roof and watch him throw sticks and wet leaves down onto the front garden. I look at all the other leaves and sticks thrown there on every other Saturday and, again, I think that the eavestroughs must have had something to do with my mother's leaving.

"Emily?"

"Now you put the car in reverse." I show Joe how to do it and he does it and we jerk slowly out of the driveway and stall in the road.

"Let your foot off the clutch slowly. It's like a see-saw, one foot up, one foot down."

Joe smiles. He looks at where the car was and where it is now and he smiles. Then he starts singing some stupid rap song about being "baaad, oh yeah, baaad."

I am seventeen years old and I am teaching my third boyfriend in eight months how to drive my father's car. I have only eight weeks left of grade eleven and my mother moved out three weeks ago.

I watch Joe sing and I watch my father pull out sticks and throw them down to the ground. I put my head in my hands.

A car comes up behind us and beeps.

"What do I do? What do I do?" Joe panics.

"Don't panic," I say. I look down at my bare legs. I am wearing shorts. I've missed a spot shaving and so I flex that spot and watch the stubble move up and down on my leg.

The car behind us beeps again.

Joe does everything right with the car, he even puts it in neutral to start it, but then he puts it in reverse and we smash into the people behind us. We smash into them and then we stall. Their horn goes off and Joe slumps down in the seat and puts his head on the steering wheel.

I look up.

In the side mirror I can see the people, a man and a woman, getting out of their car. The woman's arms are flailing around wildly. The man is red-faced and big and beefy. Joe groans.

I got a postcard from my mother yesterday. It was from British Columbia, somewhere on the island. I got it out of the mail before my father came home and, after I read it, I tore it into pieces and flushed it down the toilet. Now, for some reason, I can't remember anything about the postcard. I can't remember her message, or the picture, or where exactly she is. I'm even starting to wonder if I actually got a postcard or if I just made it all up.

Joe climbs out of the car. My father makes his way down the ladder and walks towards us. He is stiff from crouching on the roof and his legs are bowed from years of playing goalie on my uncle's hockey team. He comes at us like an ape, his arms swinging loosely at his sides, his hair dishevelled by the wind, and he says what he always says in situations like this. He says, "What's the problem here?" and then Joe starts talking and the man and woman wave their arms around and my father looks down into the car window and straight at me and holds his hand up like a crossing guard.

"Stop," he says. "Stop talking. Can't you see my daughter's hurt?"

My father reaches down, opens the door, crouches beside me and holds me. He puts his large arms around my shoulders, and, only when he does that do I realize that I am shaking.

"I'm not hurt," I say. "Really, I'm OK."

My father hugs me hard and then lets go and shuts the door to the car. I sit in the car watching Joe explain himself. When he points to me and says that I'm not a very good teacher I know that our relationship is over. Then something inside of me clicks and I remember that there was a lonely-looking moose standing beside a blue-green lake on my mother's postcard. A lonely, old moose and some trees and a mountain and a lake.

Canadian stuff.

Touristy stuff.

I slide slowly and quietly into the driver's side and I start the car and zoom off down the street leaving everyone standing there. From the rearview mirror I can see the woman's arms still waving frantically. The man she's with is pointing at me. He looks like he is going to explode.

Driving away from there I feel crazy and free. All I can think about are those driving lessons my father paid for and how the first thing you learn is to never, ever leave the scene of an accident. The second thing you learn is to never, ever drive without your seatbelt on.

I look down at my seatbelt. It is loose. It is flapping around with the gusts of air from the open window. I turn right on Main Street and, as I drive in no particular direction, I shout along with the music on the car stereo.

The songs beat rhythmically, mix with my shouts and rush out the window, into the open air.

Directions: How to Get There from Here

"How did you get here from your place?" Joan asks.

"I took Avondale north until Highway 6. Then I went west for about half a kilometre until Crescent Street. There's a stoplight there. And a 7-Eleven. I think there may be a gas station on the south side of the street. Anyway, if you go this way, you come up almost at Keyhole Avenue . . ."

Jim's voice is soft, but staccato. The words bounce from his lips like rain. I close my eyes and swallow a mouthful of beer. If I concentrate, letting my mind wander over the noise of the jukebox, I can hear the rain falling on the cars in the parking lot just outside the bar. It has been raining hard off and on for about two hours now and the cars in the parking lot look shiny and new.

"I came a completely roundabout way then," Joan says. She takes a deep drag on her cigarette. "I went up Highway 12 until Avondale, then I made a quick jog over to Pipeline Drive and then a left onto Crescent Street. I came up on the south side of Crescent, but at least I avoided Highway 6."

I am sitting between Jim and Joan on one of the bar stools

in the Red Rooster Bar and Steakhouse. The Red Rooster is on Keyhole Avenue and Georgetown Crescent. I don't know which of these routes I would take to get here. Jim is the one who drives, or sometimes, if I'm meeting Joan somewhere like this by myself, I just take a bus. I read on the bus, so I don't pay much attention to directions. I know that, to get home from Joan's house, I take the #14 bus to the subway station and then I go south on the green line until Cowerthan. Then I only have to walk about a block down Cowerthan towards our apartment. Sometimes, late at night when the buses stop running and I'm feeling nervous, like someone's watching me, I take a cab home. Then I tell the driver to take me to Sandalwood Apartments on Cowerthan and Stiles. The cab driver always knows the area and usually takes me there quickly and efficiently, no questions asked.

In the window just behind the bar, I can see the parking lot and all the clean, glossy cars. The rain is falling in sheets. This parking lot is for patrons of the Red Rooster, but also for people who are shopping in Sammy Greengrocers on the other side of Keyhole Avenue. A large, red-lettered sign on a post in the lot says:

> Patron Parking
> Red Rooster Bar & Steakhouse,
> Sammy Greengrocers
> ONLY.

Even though these are the only two businesses for blocks, the ONLY has been capitalized. Someone wrote "FUCK YOU," also in capitals, right after "Greengrocers." It is written with a thick, black, felt-tip pen, the kind you see in the grocery store, near the nine-items-or-less check-out stand, selling for about $1.59. I wonder if the "FUCK YOU" is personal. I wonder if Sammy the greengrocer has any enemies. Maybe it's just another random act of violence.

Miss Trainer, back in high school, once told me I had committed a "random act of violence." I had a black-ink pen and I wrote "Jim plus Ruthie" all over the second-floor bathroom walls. I don't really know what I meant by "plus"; I don't know if, by adding us up, I made us into one, or if by putting us together in a mathematical equation I was creating something I thought I might have wanted. All I know is that "plus" was how you wrote it, and I wrote it all over the walls. I never really thought of this act as "random," or even "violent," but Miss Trainer thought it was and so I was expelled for six whole weeks. My mother still doesn't let me forget. It was the first thing she told Jim's parents when she met them at our wedding reception.

"How would you get to Betty's from here?" Jim asks Joan.

"Oh, that's easy! You just go down Trafalgar Road until you get to Duffly Street. Duffly turns into Blackholm Place just past Rideau Boulevard . . ." Betty is Joan's cousin. Jim had a crush on her in high school but she was two grades ahead of us and so she didn't know Jim existed. Now Betty is a social worker with two kids and a golden retriever. Her husband left her for another woman and Jim says she's gotten lumpy. I think he means dumpy.

Looking out the window, I see a man coming out of Sammy's with a bag full of groceries, a couple of vegetables riding precariously close to the edge. In his left hand he is carrying one of those plastic-wrapped, leafy plants—you know, the kind that usually has a tiny stuffed teddy bear buried somewhere beneath the leaves—the kind of plant you would give to someone who just had a baby. This is one of those plants. It falls into the same category as the plants that are growing in porcelain baby boots and little pink lambs. Anyway, this man isn't in much of a hurry even though the rain is falling quickly and the plant looks heavy. He steps delicately over the puddles, moving around several large ones, a newspaper carefully balanced like a pup tent over his head. I watch as he climbs into one of the cleanest cars in the lot, the kind of car that was clean even before the rain. He adjusts his seatbelt, puts the plant carefully down on the passenger seat, and starts the engine.

Joan clears her throat and fiddles with her gold earrings. Her cigarette is long and slim. I notice a mascara-covered eyelash sticking awkwardly to her cheek, just above her upper lip, but I'm feeling too slow and comfortable to move towards her and knock it off.

"What about if you wanted to get from Betty's over to my house?" Jim asks Joan. "Can you still take Duffly?"

Joan sips at her white wine, nodding her head to Jim's question. "It's really simple. All you do is take Trafalgar to Rideau, just before Duffly. Then go south on Rideau until Stiles."

"I didn't know Stiles went all the way to Rideau!" Jim is amazed. He orders us all more drinks.

Joan's car sits between the yellow parking lines right underneath the sign that says "FUCK YOU." She left her parking lights on. I can see them getting brighter as the day fades. I pull at my hair, a habit my mother says I developed in grade school, and think hard of telling her about this.

I can't see our van from where I'm sitting. I've forgotten where Jim parked it because I had my eyes closed. I like to close my eyes when Jim's driving, or when anyone's driving for that matter. It's not just that I like to close my eyes: for some reason, I can't really stop closing them. My father used to say that the car's vibration would hypnotize me when I was a kid. He used to put me in the car and turn on the engine, just to get me to sleep at night. That's why I don't drive. I imagine my eyes involuntarily closing as I barrel down Rideau or Highway 10.

"I went to the Town Plaza last night, Ruthie, to buy a pair of sandals. I figured that, with summer just over, the sales would be fantastic." Joan turns to blow smoke in my face. I smile at her and pretend I am interested. I am still watching myself crash into the guardrails on Rideau; with my eyes tightly closed the car crumples around me. I think about what Joan just said and I can't help looking down at her feet. "Oh, silly, I'm not wearing them today," she says and pokes at my arm. I rub the spot where she poked and glance again at her pointed, well-polished shoes. "How'd you get there from your place? Dawklin Road and Number 47?" Jim swigs at his beer and stares intently into Joan's eyes. The eyelash has fallen off her cheek and I look for it on the shiny surface of the bar. "Oh no. You'd get stuck in traffic if you went that way. I took Number 46 and Highway 2. Then I went west on . . ."

I look back out at the almost deserted parking lot and think of Joan back in high school. She was the first to pass her driving test. I remember going with her when her father took her to practise. We'd drive around and around Circle Road up by the university, Joan staring intently at the road, her father clutching the door handle. I'd be in the back thinking about Jim. I used to like watching the trees and the buildings and the university pass by. Everything would loom solidly in the distance, approach rapidly and then disappear as we drove around and around the circle. After awhile my eyes would close and all I could see was Jim's large face.

As Joan talks about the mall, I reach over and curl my fingers over Jim's hand. I squeeze. Hard. It's been a long time since we went shopping. I'm trying to get this message through his thick fingers and up into his brain. He glances at me and pulls his fingers out from under mine. I've broken his concentration.

"You want another beer, Ruthie?" he asks and signals to the bartender before I even answer.

Jim used to ask my dad how to get places: the driving range, the ocean, the tennis courts. But we'd always end up in some deserted park, making love in the folded-back seat of his father's station wagon.

He had this way with his hands and his fingers.

"How was golfing?" my father would ask when I came home.

41

Jim smiles at something Joan is saying. I take a large swallow of the beer that Jim places in front of me and I slouch down on my stool. I'm tired and I'm full and I have to pee. I watch as another man walks out of Sammy's and stands under the awning. He puts his hand out to feel the rain and then trots quickly to his car. His car is dented and rusty, the kind of car that never looks clean, even in rain. He fumbles in his coat pocket for the keys. His hand moves over his clothing, into his pants pocket, his vest, back to his coat. He switches his grocery bag into his other hand and then searches his remaining pockets. The rain is falling hard. Then, like in cartoons, a lightbulb goes on over his head. I swear I can see it. He looks into his car. I can imagine his eyes moving up to the steering wheel and over to the ignition. He sees his keys. The man begins to smash his hand against the hood of the car. The rain has soaked through his hair and his coat.

"There was a gruesome accident on the 501 the other day. A woman was hit head-on. She was killed instantly and her body supposedly shot out of the broken windshield and onto the highway. It stopped traffic for miles around."

I imagine a rag-doll body jerking around on the highway. A knot of tension travels down my spine. I shiver, flexing my shoulders.

"I know!" says Joan. "I got stuck in it. I had this huge meeting I had to get to in Burmham and I didn't know which way to turn!" She lights up another cigarette and I watch as her fading lipstick stains the filter—little wrinkled, pursed pink lips.

"Did you take the turnabout to Highway 4 or the exit onto the 602?" Jim asks.

"Well, I'll tell you what I did. I discovered this little route through . . ."

The man has disappeared from beside his car. He has left his grocery bag underneath the car where it's dry and safe. I look towards Sammy Greengrocers and can see him through the well-lit window. He is waving his arms to somebody. I see a hand handing him something. He comes out seconds later with a clothes hanger in one hand and jogs through the puddles towards his car. He pushes the clothes hanger down the inside of his car window. The rain has picked up and the wind is howling. A fast-food carton rushes past him. The man's face is red. His beige coat has turned dark—a large wet stain is travelling in a V from his neck to his lower back.

The parking lights on Joan's car slowly dim and then go out.

I remember when Jim left me stranded on top of Look-Out Hill. It was dark and cold and I walked quickly down the hill towards my parents' house.

Even though I was only about two blocks from my house, I was afraid I'd get lost.

"How did you get to the polling centre, Ruthie?" Joan asks me. "Oh, God," she apologizes, "I forgot—you don't drive."

"She didn't go," Jim says. "I couldn't get off work early enough to pick her up. Ruthie didn't vote."

I smile at Joan. "Wouldn't be the first time, eh?"

She laughs and taps her long, painted nails against the bar. She pulls out a compact and some lipstick and begins to touch up her mouth.

"I still don't understand why you haven't got your licence, Ruthie," she says with a frown.

I shrug.

The man outside has managed to open his car door. He is sitting in the driver's seat playing with the clothes hanger. The door of the car is open and the engine is running. I can see the exhaust coming out the back of the car and dispersing quickly in the wind. He puts his head in his hands and begins to shake. All of a sudden he slams the car door and drives off. His bag of groceries sits in the one dry spot in the parking lot. I watch as it slowly gets wetter and wetter. I watch as the bag breaks, spilling its contents. A tomato rolls away from the other vegetables. Soon the outline of the car is gone. The rain has washed it away.

I climb down from my bar stool and head towards the washroom.

The stalls in here are painted black. Someone has sponged white paint on top of the dried black. The effect is spooky, like when you shine a flashlight through a spider's web. I am crouching over the toilet, trying not to touch the seat. Someone has written on the toilet seat and I have to swivel my head to read the writing: "Don't piss on the seat."

I read it again after I've finished peeing and then I wipe the seat with some rolled-up toilet paper.

After that time on Look-Out Hill Jim didn't talk to me for several months. I was getting pretty heavy by that time and I was beginning to wonder how long I could go on like that. I used to go for walks every night with my mom. Just around the neighbourhood. We memorized a certain route and we never went a different direction. I'd lived in the same neighbourhood my entire life, but I was still afraid of getting lost.

Jim finally stopped me in the cafeteria and said we had to talk. I figured that he had finally made up his mind to do the right thing, that he would marry me and we'd have the kid.

Sometimes, though, there isn't much satisfaction in being right.

Ours was a quick wedding. Afterwards, my dad had several drinks with Jim and then he got out the rifle.

"What's a wedding in this family without a shotgun?" he shouted and everyone laughed.

I am washing my hands in the sink. It has those new faucets that come on automatically. You just move your hands under the tap and, bingo, there's water. The dryers are like that too.

I run my hands back and forth under a dryer, playing with

the motion sensors. The clicking of the dryer going off and on, the whir of the heaters and fans, is all pretty relaxing. I close my eyes and imagine everything in the world controlled by small sensors—the washing machine, the dishwasher, the television, the stove. As I leave the washroom, I move my hand rapidly under the long line of dryers, setting off each sensor, sending each dryer into a whirring, blowing frenzy.

Jim and Joan are now facing each other. I don't know where to sit, so I stand up behind my stool and order another beer.

"God, the meeting was horrendous! Taylor couldn't believe that Arrelco would fold under. He always said, 'Arrelco will never fold!' and then it did. It shocked the hell out of him."

Jim and Joan work for the same company. The company builds and repairs car stereos. Joan is a secretary and Jim's in the factory. They have both been there since high school.

"I swear it was the location of Arrelco. Who the hell wants to drive all the way out to Trendway to get their car stereo fixed?"

"But Taylor said their warranties were really good. Sometimes five or six years, depending on the make." Joan shakes her cigarette container. It is empty.

It is beginning to get really dark outside and the rain still hasn't stopped. Sammy Greengrocers is closing up for the night. I can see someone in a green apron (Sammy himself?) moving about in the store, pushing a broom or a mop around. He pulls the blinds down purposefully, as if he knows someone is watching.

Jim looks into my face and then quickly looks away. "Where were you?" he asks.

"In the bathroom."

He rubs his hand up and down my back, but he still doesn't look into my eyes.

"Why don't you sit down?"

I move onto my stool and settle down like a giant hen on her roost. I can feel the spread of my bum on the seat.

"God, I'm getting fat," I say.

"Don't be silly," Joan says, quickly. She is rehearsed at answers like that. She is, after all, a woman.

Jim just looks at me.

"Drink white wine," he says. "It's supposed to have less calories than beer."

I nod.

Jim orders a large plate of chicken wings and then begins to play with his napkin in nervous anticipation.

"You still sleeping with Taylor?" he asks suddenly.

Joan looks shocked. "Who told you about that?"

I look down at my feet. I'm wearing running shoes. The swelling took so long to go away after the kid was born and I couldn't get my feet into anything other than running shoes. I guess I just got used to wearing them.

"I was on my way to work the other morning," Jim says, "and I took the shortcut down Waverly, past your apartment. I saw Taylor's car just ahead of me and I followed him to work. He kept looking into his rearview mirror to adjust his tie and wipe his face, but he didn't see me."

"She told you, didn't she?" Joan glares at me.

"No. I never did, Joan." I feel like shouting but I don't. "I didn't even know Jim knew."

We all sit quietly for a minute. Joan tugs and rips her cigarette package into tiny pieces.

"It was a one-night thing," Joan says, finally.

"Yeah, whatever," Jim says and his chicken wings arrive. "You'd think he could have left earlier, or even left through the alley."

Joan shrugs. "I guess he could've gone out the alley and then taken Highway 2," she says.

"Or even Route 106," Jim says. His mouth is full of chicken and he looks like a child with his cheeks all puffed out.

"Would you mind, honey?" Joan pushes some change at me and signals towards the cigarette machine.

I walk over to the machine, past the jukebox and the pool table, and I push in the change. One, two, three, four. . . . It's getting expensive to smoke these days.

I'm thinking of the kid playing with his blocks. He likes to pretend he's Jim and move things around in all sorts of directions on the floor. I pull out a cigarette from Joan's pack and stick it in between my lips. I stopped smoking after I had the kid and he was born underweight. I look at the cigarettes. I bought Matinee by accident, Joan smokes du Maurier.

I breathe in my cigarette and move over towards the window. I'm trying to remember my life before Jim, but I can't. The night has closed in and all I can see is my reflection in the large, black window. I have to push my face up close and peer out into the dark hole. Sammy Greengrocers is just an outline in the black. The bag of groceries lies scattered all over the parking lot, and I can see the wind ripping at a box of something, maybe cookies. The box is moving slowly away from all the other groceries, towards the tomato. I pull away from the window and suck in on the cigarette. Smoke curls around my head and steams up the window. Some smoke goes in my nose and travels down the wrong tube in my throat. I cough. I feel a hand on my shoulder.

"What are you doing?" Jim asks.

"Nothing," I say and offer him a cigarette from Joan's pack. I'm hoping he'll go away so I can concentrate.

"Thanks," Jim says and takes the whole pack. He puts his hand on my shoulder lightly, but I shrug him off. He walks back to the bar.

I look back out the window and everything seems suddenly quiet. The jukebox disappears and the laughter and the talking and the sounds of the bar. All I can hear are the wind and the rain. If I push my head right up against the window I can almost feel the rain and the wind thrash against my body. I'm still trying hard to remember my life before Jim. I can remember my mother and father clearly, I remember their large, soft faces, but I can't remember myself. I try floating out of my body and looking down on who I was. I try to see the whole picture.

An image of myself as a young girl is pushed into my mind by the wind and the rain. I open my eyes. There I am, thirteen, maybe fourteen, walking through the streets of the city, all alone. Alone. This was before Jim. Before the kid. I am not afraid. I'm not going to get lost.

I smile and the image disappears. All I can see now is the box of cookies stuck in a puddle. The water eats into the box and it begins to dissolve.

"Ruthie?" Joan calls to me. I walk back to the bar.

Joan is smoking her cigarettes. She doesn't say anything about the brand. Jim offers us some chicken wings and we both dig in. We are all silent except for the occasional sucking sound when we lick our fingers.

"Did you call the babysitter?" Jim asks between bites.

"No, I forgot." I stare at our reflections in the window.

Jim sighs and carries his beer slowly over to the pay phone in the corner of the bar.

For some reason I am feeling really hungry. I can't stop eating the chicken wings. Joan stops eating and wipes her fingers on a napkin. She lights up another cigarette. I'm famished. I'm starved. The chicken can't fill me up, and I think of that box of cookies, that tomato. I wonder what else is in that bag. Joan looks at me and grins. I grin back. Juice from the chicken is dripping down my chin but I don't care. Joan looks around for Jim. My mind is moving as fast as my mouth. As I chew I think about tomorrow and the day after, about walking around the city, around and around. By myself. God, I think, God, I just want to get around. I just want to move around, I think, around and around. I begin to chuckle a bit. Jim has come back and I can hear Joan say, "I think the beer has gone to her head." I laugh.

"All I want," I say, "is a few directions. Right? I mean, how would you get there from here?"

The Glass Piano

"*How come* doesn't mean anything, Jeff. Stop saying *how come*."

"But how come she thought she swallowed the glass piano?" Jeff poked her knees. His hand was tender but insistent. He needed to know so badly he was going to burst. He felt like he did just before he went to the bathroom. As soon as he knew he would be all right.

"Try saying, *Why did she think she swallowed the glass piano?* Saying *how come* is just plain vulgar." Celia's hands were shaking as she tried to light her cigarette. She looked down at Jeff but all she could think about was how rotten her head felt. She tried to smile but it was too hard and so she gave up.

"Why? Why?" Jeff said, loudly.

Celia's arms ached from carrying the dishes inside after the party and her brain felt rotten. Like rotten cheese, she thought. All Celia wanted to do was to vomit. She wanted to retch into the toilet and clear her stomach of all that vile whisky she'd been drinking all afternoon. Never again, she kept saying in her rotten head, never, never again.

Instead of throwing up, however, Celia was in Bobby's living room, in a white, silk bathrobe, talking to his nine-year-old son and feeling very nervous. She was sitting, half-leaning, on the white leather sofa, smoking. Jeff stood in front of her, beside her crossed knees. When the ashes from her cigarette dropped into the folds of the sofa Jeff wiped them carefully onto the floor. Celia jumped every time he touched the sofa.

Celia couldn't remember where Bobby went. He had disappeared just before Jeff had entered the room. He's probably retching, Celia thought. God, he is probably throwing up somewhere.

"Was the piano large or small? What kind of piano was it? You shouldn't start a story and not finish it."

"Shouldn't you be somewhere else?" Celia asked. "Shouldn't you be in bed or at your mother's?"

"This is not that weekend," Jeff said. "This is the other weekend."

Celia rubbed her temples.

"I'll go to bed after you tell me about that crazy woman," Jeff said. "I promise I'll leave after you tell me how come."

His finger reached out to poke Celia and she smacked it lightly. She sighed and closed her eyes. She was beginning to feel faint. She wished he would just go away. "It was a piano. Just a piano. But it was glass." Celia couldn't think of anything else to say. As a matter of fact, she was quickly forgetting what they were talking about.

Jeff hadn't. He stood in front of her, close up. His breath reeked of toothpaste. "What would a glass piano look like anyway?" he said.

Celia pushed his face away. "You are much too close," she said. "Much, much too close."

Jeff backed up. "Well, I'll stand on your toes if you don't tell me. I'll spit in your face."

"If you were my child," Celia threatened, but then couldn't think of what she would do if he were her child. She didn't want to think about it.

"Where is your father?" she asked. "Go ask your father

about the glass piano. He knows better than I do. He watched the show from start to finish."

"I can't believe Dad didn't call me at Mom's and wake me. I can't believe he let me sleep through this show. I can't believe it." Jeff moved close to Celia again and glared into her face. "Tell me how come!" he shouted. Celia jumped.

The room moved around in circles in Celia's rotten cheese head. "Where is your father?"

Jeff moved back again and looked over his shoulder. "I don't know where he is," he said. He looked at Celia again. "Did she really swallow a little glass piano or did she just think she did?" And then Jeff whispered more to himself than to Celia, "I can't even imagine a piano made of glass."

Celia sighed and took a deep breath. At least he isn't standing so close anymore, she thought.

"Get me some water and I'll tell you everything I know," she said.

Jeff rushed out of the room, his open bathrobe billowing out behind him.

"Bobby!" Celia shouted into the still house. "Come out here this instant!"

When Jeff returned he was carefully carrying a large glass of water. He sat down beside Celia and poked at her knees again.

"Stop that. Just stop poking me. Don't touch me."

Celia gulped from the water glass. This child is insane, she thought. If this child were mine, she thought, I'd throw him out with the garbage. I'd give him away.

"She was a princess of some sort. I think she must have been the king's cousin or something because he was an only child. Or maybe he wasn't, I don't know. I don't know much about this. Wouldn't it be better if you asked your father and just left me alone?" Celia looked down at Jeff. She wished he was at his mother's house. He was usually at his mother's house.

Jeff just looked at her. He didn't go away.

"She was crazy, Jeff. The announcer said that she thought she swallowed a glass piano. I don't know the size of the piano.

I don't know if it was a miniature one or a large one or what. But she thought she swallowed one and she went completely insane."

"That doesn't tell me anything," Jeff said. "I mean, maybe she did swallow a glass one and no one believed her. Maybe it was a tiny, itsy bitsy one like this." Jeff held up the palm of his hand and measured out an inch or two.

"Well, that's all I know," Celia said. "I only watched the last bit of the show. I don't know what happened to her."

Jeff sat there. He didn't know what else to say. He got up from the couch and turned towards the door. He started to say something.

"Good night," Celia said. She tried to smile at him as he exited the room but all she came up with was a grimace.

"Oh, Jeff?"

Jeff poked his head back into the living room.

"I think they committed her. I think the Bavarian government put her in a mental hospital."

"Oh," Jeff said and then left the room.

"Her whole family was crazy," Celia said to herself. "Absolutely insane."

Celia fell asleep on the sofa just for a minute. Her legs popped further out of the white silk bathrobe.

"Wake up," Bobby said when he finally came into the living room. "Wake up, Celia." He still felt drunk.

"What?" she mumbled and then woke up. "Where have you been?"

"I got rid of those awful drinks," Bobby said. "You should do the same. You'd feel much better."

"You know I can't do that," Celia said. She rose up into a sitting position. "I can't bear to stick my finger in my throat."

"I'll do it for you," Bobby said and put his finger up to her lips.

"That's disgusting, Bobby," Celia said. She tried to push his hand away but she suddenly felt like she didn't have any strength. She couldn't even light her cigarette. Bobby reached for the lighter and lit it for her. She sucked in the smoke and then exhaled, leaving the cigarette dangling from her lips.

"What time is it?" she asked.

"Eleven-thirty," Bobby said. "Can you believe it's only eleven-thirty? I feel like I've been up all night."

Bobby cuddled up to Celia and took the cigarette from her lips. "Give me some," he said and took a puff.

"We started drinking at lunch," Celia said. "I don't think I'll ever drink at lunch again."

"Hmmm." Bobby looked out through the smoke of his cigarette into the living room.

"Wake up, Bobby," she said. "Don't you fall asleep on me now." She gave him a playful punch.

"I'm awake," he said. "Just thinking about lunch. Just thinking about . . ." He drifted off.

Celia poked him. "What were you and Sylvia talking about?" she asked. "What were you two whispering about out there?"

"Nothing." Bobby pulled at the cigarette and then blew rings into the air. "She was just telling me about Richard," he said.

"What about him?" Celia pulled her bathrobe shut and straightened her body on the sofa. The leather squeaked below her. "Well, what about him?"

Bobby moved towards the arm of the sofa and rested his head. "Honestly, Celia, I just don't know. I can't remember now. That was so long ago."

For a moment there was complete silence. Celia looked confused.

Then Celia said, "Shit, Bobby. You left me here with him. He came out and talked and talked."

"He doesn't bite, Celia," Bobby said. "He's just a little boy."

"God, he talks and talks. He doesn't stop poking me!"

"What did you talk about?" Bobby asked.

"I told him about the Fairy-Tale King's crazy cousin. The one in Bavaria who thought she swallowed the glass piano. Remember? We saw it on TV the other day?"

"That was nice of you," Bobby said. "But I think that was his sister, wasn't it?" He was drifting off.

"Wake up, Bobby!" Celia pulled at his feet. "I don't know who it was. I wasn't really watching the show, remember? But that's not the point. The point is, you left me here with him and that makes me feel uncomfortable. I told you never to do that. I told you."

"I had to throw up, Celia. What did you want me to do?"

Celia looked over at Bobby. He was staring at her.

"You could lock him in his room or something," she said. "He gives me the creeps. He's always poking me and asking questions. And he is so god-damned rude. Didn't you two teach him any manners?"

Bobby kept staring at Celia. He lit another cigarette.

"I mean, why isn't he at his mother's? Why didn't she take him? I thought that was our deal. I thought I would be here and he wouldn't be." Celia was almost crying.

"I can't believe you, Celia," Bobby said. "Frannie had to go to her mother's house. She had an operation last week and Frannie thought it would be nice if she took care of her mother. I just don't believe you, Celia. He is my child. He is my son. Get used to it."

"I didn't mean that," she said. "Honest. I just feel like shit."

"He is my son," Bobby said again, loudly. "I think he's smart and neat. I think he's special." Bobby stopped and then whispered, "I think you're a bitch sometimes."

Celia pulled her bathrobe around her tightly and got up from the sofa.

"I think you're right, Bobby. I think that was uncalled for. I'm sorry," she said. "I'm going to bed."

Celia walked out of the living room and went up the stairs. She stumbled slightly. She was crying.

"Fine with me," Bobby said to the air and then sucked deeply on his cigarette. "That's just fine with me."

Bobby sat alone in the living room for awhile. He thought about the glass piano. He couldn't imagine if the princess thought she had swallowed a large one—which made absolutely no sense—or if she thought she had swallowed one of those small toy ones. He came to the conclusion that she had probably imagined the large one or else why would they have put her in a mental hospital. But then he thought about the luncheon party and about how Sylvia had told him things he really didn't want to know about Celia. Things about Celia's past; some child her parents made her give up for adoption when she was sixteen; some nervous breakdown she had; some hospital she was in; things Celia had never told him; things he knew nothing about. No matter how hard he thought about it, Bobby couldn't understand why Sylvia had told him these things. Just out of the blue. She just up and told him out of the blue.

And then he thought about how furious Sylvia had made him, almost mad enough to kill, and then Bobby thought that just about anything could make you go completely crazy these days.

"I've been thinking about it," Jeff said the next morning at breakfast. He was sitting across from Celia and Bobby at the breakfast table.

Celia and Bobby barely glanced at Jeff. Bobby's neck ached from sleeping on the sofa. He sat at the table, pretending to read the paper but really thinking about what Sylvia had said and about how he was going to ask Celia if any of it was true.

"I've been thinking about the piano stuff," Jeff said. "I thought about it all last night." He put down his cereal spoon and looked about the table, waiting for an audience.

"Hmmm," Bobby said. Celia glanced up from her cigarette and her coffee. She smiled as politely as she could at Jeff. She even tried to show her teeth. She wasn't used to someone, some child, talking at the breakfast table.

Jeff cleared his throat several times. He waited.

"Well?" Bobby said. He put down the newspaper and stared at his son. He knew he would have to hear him out. "Tell us what you figured out."

Jeff looked back and forth between the two grown-ups. "I think that it is really possible to believe in something that isn't there. I think that lots of people believe in things that don't really happen and nobody can know what the other person really feels. I don't think she was crazy at all."

"But was it a large piano or a small one?" Celia asked.

"I think it was a large one. Solid glass, even the keys were glass. I think that she imagined that her mouth was really big and she swallowed it all in one gulp. I think she was probably in a lot of pain, keeping all that piano inside of her." Jeff stopped talking and looked back and forth from Celia to Bobby. "What do you guys think?" he asked.

"I think that you are about the smartest boy alive," Celia said without stopping to think first. She smiled. She was being honest. She was really trying.

"Thanks," Jeff said.

Bobby looked from Jeff to Celia. He thought about that glass piano, the one Jeff had described. He thought about the princess and how she had swallowed it in one big gulp. Then he wondered why the princess had told anyone. He thought that if she hadn't said anything they wouldn't have known. Then they wouldn't have put her away.

Bobby took Celia's hand, carried it to his mouth, and kissed it hard.

"He is smart," Celia said. "He is so smart he makes me want to vomit." She giggled.

"Don't be so vulgar," Jeff said and then he smiled shyly.

"How come?" Celia said and then she smiled widely. "How come? How come?"

Jeff began to giggle. He said "Why?" and then giggled even harder. Celia laughed with him. Jeff laughed so hard he spilt his cereal on the table. Celia laughed.

Bobby just looked at the two of them from behind Celia's hand. He couldn't let go of her, he couldn't stop kissing her hand.

When they had stopped laughing, Celia touched Jeff's arm with her other hand and said, "It would take an awfully long time for someone to heal after swallowing a glass piano, wouldn't it, Jeff?"

Do You Know
Who Emily Carr Is?

*J*oe was sitting behind the front desk thinking. He thought for awhile. He watched the rain stream down the windows. It was a Tuesday and it was raining. They were the first people to come in.

"Welcome to the gallery," Joe said.

"Hello," said the woman. The little girl put her chin out like an ape.

Joe reached down to pat the little girl's head. He reached down and smoothed her hair. It was soft, thick hair. The girl stopped making her face and moved quickly behind the woman. She stared up at Joe. Joe didn't know what made him do that, touch her like that, but touching her hair made him feel ill. He shuffled his feet. The woman didn't say anything. She moved her head around like an injured bird and clutched at the little girl's school uniform. When Joe thought back on it later, it all made sense.

"Would you like to see the gallery?" he asked after awhile. They were just standing there.

The little girl moved away from the woman and did a little jig. Joe realized she was dancing. Her arms moved up and down and her feet moved all around. It looked as if she was running against the wind. Joe clapped when she was finished.

The woman looked at Joe. She handed him some money. Her hands were shaking and the money was wet from the rain.

"Tickets, please," the woman said.

"The girl is free," Joe said as he smoothed the money flat with a pencil and placed it carefully in the cash register.

The woman nodded. "Yes, I guess she is," she said and then looked down at her feet.

"Do you know who Emily Carr is?" Joe asked the little girl after he handed them their tickets. He didn't want to stop talking to them. It was raining and his stomach was beginning to feel better. He liked the way the little girl danced.

He watched as they walked up the stairs into the first room. They stood side by side, looking around. Joe watched as the woman bent down and whispered to the little girl. They moved over and stood in front of a fourteenth-century Sienese painting of the Madonna and child. The little girl traced the baby Christ's arm in the air. His fat little arm was stretched straight across the middle of the painting, his baby fingers jammed into the Madonna's mouth. The little girl traced his arm, his fingers, the mouth and then she sighed. Joe could hear her sigh.

At that moment Joe was distracted. He looked away. When he looked back the two figures were kneeling in front of the picture, bowing their heads.

"Christ," Joe said.

Seeing them up there, kneeling on the floor, made Joe uncomfortable. He couldn't imagine what they were doing. He stared at them for awhile. The little girl opened her big eyes and looked down the stairs at Joe. She stuck out her tongue. Joe felt like he'd been shot. The woman's lips were moving. Joe wished he could hear what the woman was saying. He wished he could know what she was praying for.

The gallery was empty. The rain came down hard. Joe tried humming but that didn't work. He tried pacing in front of his desk. They just kneeled there. Joe felt really sick. He felt like something was going to happen.

The Most Peculiar Thing

*J*oe was sitting behind the front desk thinking. He thought for awhile of his baby daughter who was six months old. And then he cleared his mind and thought of nothing in particular. He watched the rain stream down the windows and pondered the effect of water on glass. That's when he first saw them come in. It was a Tuesday and it was raining and they were the first people to come in. Joe stood up quickly and smiled.

"Welcome to the art gallery," he said.

"Hello," the woman said as she approached his desk. The little girl put her chin out like an ape and then grinned widely.

"Hello," the child echoed. And then she said something else. "We've just come from my school. We just walked out together." She laughed and looked up at the woman.

Joe couldn't help but smile and then he laughed out loud and reached down to pat the little girl's head. He reached down and smoothed her hair. It was soft and thick. He imagined that Beth would be like this girl when she grew up. The second he touched her hair the girl stopped making her face and moved quickly behind the woman. She stared up at him strangely. Joe didn't know what made him do that, touch her like that, but touching her made him feel peculiar and a little ill. He felt like he did in the morning after a night out; his stomach like acid, his throat itchy, his brain blurry and loud. He shuffled his feet, feeling awkward. The woman didn't say anything to Joe but she acted strangely. She moved her head around like an injured bird and then she clutched at the little girl's school uniform. When Joe thought back on it later, it all made sense.

"Would you like to see the gallery?" he asked after a long pause. They were just standing there, staring at him, and he couldn't think of any other way to sell them a ticket.

"Oh yes," the little girl said and then she did the most peculiar thing. She moved away from the woman and did a little jig. For a minute Joe thought she was jogging on the spot. Then he realized that she was dancing. Her arms moved up and down and her feet moved all around. It looked almost as if she was running against the wind. He clapped when she was finished and the sound echoed around the gallery. She's one cute kid, Joe thought. One really cute kid.

The woman just looked at Joe and then she handed him some crumpled money. Her hands were shaking and the money was wet from the rain.

"Tickets, please," she said.

"The girl is free," Joe said as he smoothed the money flat with a pencil and placed it carefully in the cash register. The woman nodded.

"Yes, I guess she is," she said and then looked down at her feet.

"Do you know who Emily Carr is?" Joe asked the little girl after he handed them their tickets. For some reason he didn't want to stop talking to them. It was raining and his stomach was beginning to feel better. Besides, this little girl intrigued him. He liked the way she danced.

"Nope." The girl moved off, following the woman. Every once in awhile she turned towards Joe and did a little bit more of that jig. Joe just smiled even though he felt like clapping.

"Well," Joe called out. "There's a special exhibit of hers here today. Emily Carr. In the orange room. You should see it."

He watched as they walked up the stairs and into the first room. They stood there, side by side, looking around. Joe watched as the woman bent down and whispered to the little girl. Then they moved over and stood in front of a fourteenth-century Sienese painting of the Madonna and child. The little girl traced the baby Christ's arm in the air. His fat little arm was stretched straight across the middle of the painting, his baby fingers jammed into the Madonna's mouth. The little girl traced his arm, his fingers, the mouth and then she sighed. Quite loudly too. Joe could hear it from his desk at the bottom of the stairs.

At that moment Joe was distracted by Martha as she entered the gallery. But before he looked away Joe was almost certain that he saw the woman cross herself and then curtsy. He also thought that the little girl winked at him, but later, when he reflected upon it, that didn't really make any sense.

"Think it'll be slow today, Joe?" Martha asked as she folded up her umbrella. Martha had this way of asking Joe questions that made his skin crawl.

"Yeah," he said and then he looked quickly back up at the girl and the woman to see what they were doing. Martha followed his gaze.

"Shit," he whispered aloud when he saw them.

"They think they're in church or something?" Martha whispered back and then she laughed. "Did you tell them this wasn't a church, Joe?"

The two figures were kneeling in front of the picture now and bowing their heads.

"Christ," Joe said.

Martha shook her head back and forth and then walked into her office and shut the door behind her.

Seeing them up there, kneeling on the floor, made Joe uncomfortable. He couldn't imagine what they were doing. He stared at them for awhile but they didn't budge. Then he cleared his throat; still nothing. Then he tapped his fingers on the desk. The little girl opened her big eyes and looked down the stairs at Joe. She stuck out her tongue. Joe felt as though he'd been shot.

Martha needed a cup of coffee. She came out of her office with the kettle and walked over to the water fountain. Passing Joe's desk, she made a crack about putting a church pew in front of that picture.

"Maybe a chalice of holy water by the front door," she said. Joe just looked at her.

"I think we should give out Bibles tomorrow, Joe," she said. "Sing hymns, preach on Sundays." Martha was getting quite a kick out of this. Joe felt like smacking her.

Joe couldn't take his eyes off them, kneeling there, not moving. It made him feel queer inside. It made his stomach hurt and his back itch. The woman's lips moved to her silent prayer. After all that dancing, the little girl was oddly still. Joe wished he could hear what the woman was saying. He wished he could know what she was praying for. He also wished he could see the little girl dance again.

The gallery was empty. The rain came down hard. Joe tried humming but that didn't work. He tried pacing in front of his desk and coughing spasmodically. But that didn't work either. They just kneeled there, like statues. Joe felt really sick, he felt like something was going to happen. He called Amy.

"Amy, you just won't believe this," he said into the phone.

"What, Joe?" Amy sounded curious.

"I don't know how to explain it," he said. It was all he could think of saying. "How's Beth?"

"What are you talking about, Joe?" Amy asked and then she paused. "She's sleeping." Joe could suddenly hear Beth crying in the background. "Shit, Joe. The phone woke her up."

"I just had to tell you what's going on here," Joe started but then his mind went blank. He listened to his child crying on the other end of the phone. "Is she all right?"

"What's going on, Joe?" Amy said. "Tell me quickly. Beth's having a fit."

"Do you need me to come home? I might come home early," Joe said.

"No." Amy sounded frustrated.

"I'm feeling kind of sick right now," Joe said. "Is Beth all right? She's crying awfully loud. Shouldn't you get her?" Joe felt panic rising in his mouth.

"Look, Joe. Look." Amy sounded annoyed. "Just tell me what's going on there, will you."

"It's this woman and this little girl." Joe stopped.

"Amy, honey?"

"What? What, Joe?"

"I'll tell you later, OK?"

"Jesus Christ, Joe. You wake up Beth for that? Jesus Christ. Think, Joe. Think before you call." Amy hung up the phone.

Joe sat back in his chair, holding the receiver, and looked up at the girl and the woman. They were still kneeling there, bowing their heads. He could hear the dial tone clearly.

"Go do something, Joe," Martha said. She was standing behind his desk, her hands on her hips. She pointed up the stairs. "This is ridiculous."

"What?" Joe said. "What do you want me to do?"

"Tell them this isn't allowed, Joe. Tell them to go away." Martha shivered. "They make me feel creepy doing that. This is a public place, you know."

Even though Joe was feeling weird too he said, "There's no one here but us." Martha was starting to bug him.

"That's no excuse, Joe, and you know that."

She treated him as if he was a child. Sometimes he felt like killing her. Taking that thick neck between his fingers and squashing down the pipe—watching her shudder and cough. He couldn't ever imagine that she had once been a child. It boggled his mind. He tried to think of her as young and innocent. He couldn't.

"Look," Joe said. He was feeling nauseated again. "Look here."

"What, Joe?" Martha said. "What? You want them to stay there? Kneeling away, praying to a dumb painting?"

"No," Joe said.

"Well do something, for God's sake." Martha went into her office and slammed her door. Joe saw the little girl and the woman move slightly because of the noise, but then they went right back to kneeling. Joe reached under his desk and pulled out a flask. Even though he was saving it for later, when the afternoon dragged on, he took a couple of swigs, tightened the cap back on and then put it away. He felt calmer. His stomach felt settled.

Just as Joe closed the door behind his desk and walked out into the foyer, intending to go up the stairs and tell them to cut it out, two young police officers came into the gallery.

"Hello," one of them said and nodded at Joe.

Joe looked at them. Then he turned back to his desk, opened the door and settled himself behind the cash register.

"Welcome to the art gallery," he said.

"I really didn't have a clue," Joe said to Amy.

Amy was sitting at the kitchen table feeding Beth. Joe rubbed his hand over Beth's arm. The hair was soft and thick. Amy pushed his hand away.

"Let her eat," she said. Joe moved around uncomfortably.

"You couldn't tell, Joe?" Amy asked. "How could you not tell? I mean, shit, I'd be nervous as hell if I'd just killed you. I'd be shaking and stuff. Shit."

Joe looked at Amy. Beth's little hands moved rapidly in the air, clutching at the spoon in Amy's grasp.

"Beth. Quit it," Amy said.

"I'll feed her," Joe said. "Here, let me."

Amy glared at Joe and then handed him the spoon and moved out of her chair. Joe swung his hips into her chair and spooned out some creamed corn.

"Here, Beth," he said. "Eat for Daddy," he said.

"So what happened to them?" Amy asked. "What happened to the little girl after? Why'd the woman do it?"

"I don't know," Joe said. "All I know is what I said."

"I can't believe you couldn't see it, Joe. I mean, shit, how could you not see it?"

"You shouldn't swear so much around Beth, Amy."

Amy turned to wash her hands at the sink.

"I can swear as much as I damn well please." Amy said this quietly. Joe almost couldn't hear her. He decided to pretend that he hadn't.

"You should have seen Martha," Joe said. He wiped Beth's face with a damp cloth and then turned to face Amy. "I mean, imagine this, they'd been in the gallery at least a couple of hours and the woman had the gun in her bag. Right there. The murder weapon." Joe liked the sound of that phrase and so he repeated it. "The murder weapon."

"I heard you, Joe," Amy said. "Watch the baby."

Beth's fingers were on the spoon and she was tugging it towards her face.

"You're Daddy's little girl, Bethie," Joe crooned.

"Martha's a cow anyway," Amy said.

"Yeah," Joe said.

"I just can't believe you didn't see anything weird, Joe. I mean there must have been signs."

"Well, I guess there were." Joe thought about the woman and the child. "I guess if I think back on it now I can see it. But at the time . . . well, it was just all so strange. She was really nervous. I mean, she was so nervous that I was feeling sick. I phoned you, remember?"

Amy nodded. "Praying to a picture of the baby Christ in an art gallery has got to be the surest sign of something peculiar, doesn't it, Joe?"

"Yeah," Joe said. Beth finished off the creamed corn and then grabbed the spoon and knocked it on her high chair. "And that little girl was so darn happy to be out of school. That was weird, taking your kid out of school on a Tuesday. Just to go to the art gallery?" Joe paused. He took the spoon from Beth's little fingers and then patted her on the head. He smoothed her soft hair down flat.

"You know you felt sick because you drank too much last night, Joe. It had nothing to do with those people." Amy scratched Joe's scalp. She ran her fingers absently through his hair. Then she stopped. "Why didn't Martha do anything about the praying? Why didn't you guys do something?"

Joe didn't say anything. Amy clasped her arms together underneath her breasts. She leaned back on the kitchen counter.

"Well?" she asked.

Joe stared at her. He felt angry. "What should I have done, Amy? What would you have done?"

Amy thought about it for a minute. "Well, I would have asked them to leave. Asked them nicely. Told them that praying was for churches, not for art galleries. That's what I would have done."

Joe thought about that for a moment.

"The whole thing was so peculiar," Joe said. He drummed his fingers on Beth's high chair. Beth laughed.

Amy suddenly moved over to Joe and then crawled into his lap. She pushed Beth's high chair away from the table and tilted her head in close to Joe's.

"I just would've told them to cut it out," she said softly and then licked his cheek.

"Hey," he said. This kind of stuff always surprised him.

"Hey," Amy said back and then she kissed him on the lips. He kissed back hard and then reached up and touched her breasts.

"Maybe the husband was a pervert," she whispered and rubbed at Joe's chest. She unbuttoned his shirt. "Maybe he touched the little girl all over."

Joe stopped touching Amy's breasts. His fingers suddenly felt like rock.

"Hey," she said again, softly. Then Amy got up and unbuckled Beth from the high chair. She picked Beth up and carried her into the living room. She plopped her into the playpen.

"Joe," she called. "Come here."

Joe got up from the kitchen table and went into the living room. He bent down to play with Beth, but Amy took his hand and pulled him into the bedroom.

"Hey," he said.

While he was undressing Amy, pulling her pants down and unbuttoning her blouse, Joe thought about that woman and the little girl. He thought about the child mostly. About her face, how cute she was, those big eyes she had. And then he remembered that peculiar dance she had done, the jig, and he suddenly felt strange. He suddenly felt like someone had kicked him hard in the stomach. He buckled over in bed, clutching his stomach and groaning.

"Hey," Amy said. "Hey, Joe. What's wrong?"

A Familiar Tune

We are in the kitchen when she says it. It is early morning and I haven't yet got my bearings. I am sipping hot coffee and eating raisin toast. The ashtrays and wine glasses from the night before are everywhere. On the counters and on the floor. My stomach feels queasy and I have a tight headache so I can't quite understand what she says the first time. I have to ask her to repeat it twice before it really sinks in.

"Sometimes," she says. "Sometimes there are moments in a person's life when, looking back, you think you should have done something different—gone down another path, so to speak."

I just look at her, long and hard. I don't know what to say to that. I'm not the type who always knows what to say. I don't go in much for flowery speech. My first wife liked that in me. She said it showed character, made me charming and masculine and strong. Grace thinks it's just stubbornness. Grace thinks anyone can learn to say anything about everything. She thinks that being silent all the time is just a waste of a good life. "What's the point in having speech if we don't use it?" she says.

So here we are in the kitchen. I'm sitting at the table and Grace is telling me that she thinks she made all the wrong choices in her life. As I said before, it takes me a minute or two to really realize what she has said.

Grace is moving around the kitchen, straightening things. She moves the salt and pepper set from its usual place on the kitchen table to the cupboard over the stove. She dumps the ashtrays into the waste basket and then empties the wine glasses into the sink. I watch as she rinses each glass and then places it back on the counter.

"I just wonder what would have happened if we had never met," she says to the kitchen sink. "I mean, would we have been any happier? Wiser? More content? Or would we have been miserable?" She turns to look at me.

I shrug. I look at the cartoon on my coffee mug. No matter how many times I see that cartoon it still makes me laugh. There are these two pilots, in a small airplane, high up in the clouds. Peering through a cloud just in front of them is a mountain goat. The one pilot says to the other, "How'd that goat get up here in the clouds?" I chuckle. I've had this mug for six years and I still chuckle.

"I guess we probably would be just about the same, wouldn't we?" Grace says. "I guess it really doesn't matter who we're with. We are always who we are. We can't change all that much, can we?"

These questions are getting to me. I trace a finger around the mountain goat. I pour myself another cup of coffee and then I add sugar and a drop of milk. Grace turns back to the sink and begins to hum something I know I've heard before. I can't think of the words, but the tune is familiar.

I think about what Grace is saying. I wonder about her reasoning. I wonder if she's arguing just for the sake of arguing. Sometimes she does that. Like the time she packed up my duffle bag just because I looked at that girl in the park. And all the times she has been mad at me just because I don't always say the right things at the right times.

Grace fills up the kitchen sink and squirts lemon soap into

the hot water. She washes and rinses several mismatched wine glasses and then she turns back to me.

"Aren't you going to say anything, Hank?" she asks. "Are you just going to sit there, nursing your hangover, and not say anything? Don't you want to know what moments I'm talking about? What specific times in my life I wish I could have done differently?"

I was afraid she would ask me that.

"It's eight-thirty in the morning, Grace," I say. It's all I can think of saying.

"So?" Her voice is raised. She sits across from me. "So? What does the time have to do with this, Hank?"

"Listen," she says. "Just listen to me, Hank. Hear me out. Hear what I have to say."

So I do. My stomach is starting to feel a bit better so I pour another coffee and light a cigarette. I try to listen carefully to what Grace is saying. Even though I don't want to hear it, I listen anyway.

"Like the time I worked in that bar, Hank. I mean, I really wish I'd never worked there. I wish that I could have had a decent job, typing or answering phones or something like that. Instead, I poured drinks for four years and put up with the assholes and all those smart-alec remarks. I didn't say anything then, Hank. Do you understand? I kept my mouth shut back then. And then I married Joe. We had nothing in common, Hank. Nothing at all."

"You drank together," I say, just to show her I'm listening.

She looks up, starts to say something, then changes her mind.

"The point is, I really wish I never married him, but I did." Grace looks quickly at me. I nod. "And then I cheated on him, Hank. You know I did. I really wish I could take that all back because it really wasn't very nice."

Grace lights up a cigarette from my pack. She sucks on it and then turns towards the window. Her cigarette hand is shaking. I put my hand on her other one and stroke it. She has smooth, small hands.

"And there are other things I'd do differently, Hank." I watch her stand up and walk to the coffee maker. She pours me the last cup and then refills the filter and the water. When she presses the button a jet of steam comes out first and then the coffee.

For some reason my mind strays a little just then. It's the hangover. I just can't keep up with Grace this morning. I begin to think about the party last night and about Ruthie's black tights and purple dress. I can't get over how unusual she looked. Something about her was different and I can't quite put my finger on it. It's almost like she's a completely new person now. I can't stop thinking about how she moved last night, how she poured wine, how she drank wine, how she lit her cigarette. It's not that I'm still interested in her. I mean, we had some good times, but Ruthie isn't my type anymore. Besides, we've been divorced for three years and, even though we have a kid to share, we really don't have anything else in common.

"I wish I'd been nicer to my mother when she was alive," Grace is saying. "I wish that I'd known your mother and your grandmother. . . ."

Lately Grace has had this thing about mothers. She's obsessed with mothers of all types. Every time she says something it has something to do with mothers. I think she may be feeling a little left out. Sort of like she's missed her stop on the bus.

Grace has stopped talking now and she has gone back to humming that tune. Her nostrils flare and her lips purse up. She hums for awhile. Then she stops humming and starts talking again.

"Have you ever read that poem, Hank?" Grace asks. "That poem by Robert Frost about the two paths in the woods?"

"I don't think so," I say and then I think, who is she talking to? She knows I don't read poetry.

"Well, it's about two paths meeting in a wood," she says.

"You said that already," I say. I want her to know that I'm paying attention.

Grace pauses. "Well, these paths signify the different roads people take in their lives. I mean, we can choose which path we are going to take, but we can't take both of them."

"You could go back to where the two paths meet and then take the other," I say. I'm trying to be smart. It's obvious that she doesn't think I am. "I mean, if you had a compass and all."

"No, Hank. You can't go back. That's the point of the poem. You take one path and you never know what the other path would have been like."

"Well, I guess you just have to accept the path you're on or maybe even try to change it," I say. "Do some gardening, spruce it up a little. Use one of those, what do you call them, those machetes, to make it bigger."

She looks at me and her eyes widen a bit.

I start thinking about our garden and I just can't stop. I know I should be concentrating on Grace but it's a sunny day and the garden really needs some work. I have to cut the grass. It sure needs cutting. And then there are those twigs all over from that tree we pruned last year.

"That's right, Hank," Grace says, and then she gets up and finishes washing the wine glasses.

I don't really know what I've said but I've obviously impressed her. I light another cigarette and think about the conversation, the garden, my mug. I watch Grace do the dishes. Her hips sway a bit and her bathrobe starts falling off her shoulder. The white of her bare shoulder is kind of nice next to the blue of her bathrobe. I get up from the table and I kiss her naked shoulder. Then I sit down again and smoke another cigarette. My headache has gone and I'm feeling kind of hungry. I'm even feeling kind of horny right now. But when Grace finishes the dishes and turns back to me with that look the horny feeling just flies out the window.

"You know what else I wish I'd done differently?" she says and I know what's coming. "I wish I'd never even met you, Hank Johnson." Her voice is strong and rough. I sit back in my chair. Here it comes, I think. Now we'll fight all day and I won't get any gardening done. I look at that mountain goat and raise my eyebrows. It seems to me that he's looking right back at me, kind of sympathetic-like.

"Do you know why I wish I'd never met you?" she asks.

"No," I say. Her bathrobe has fallen right off that white shoulder and I can see a bit of her breast. I watch it move, even jiggle, as she talks.

"Because you never say anything, Hank. You just don't talk at all. And sometimes, Hank, sometimes I think that you just don't get it. Any of it." Grace turns and leaves the kitchen.

I sit in the kitchen for awhile. I make myself more raisin toast. I'm very careful about cleaning up the crumbs I spill on the floor. I sit there, with my toast and coffee, and I think about what a great party that was last night. I think about Edith dancing with Malcolm, how she was rubbing herself all over him and how, when they left together, Richard stormed out of the house hooting and screaming because he drank too much.

And Ruthie, boy was she drunk. She lurched all over, holding wine glasses, one red, one white, in each hand. Those purple tights. Her black dress. I can't get over how she fell into the couch with her legs in the air, laughing her head off.

I think about Grace and Bob Dickson. I think about how they spent all evening talking over in the corner by the stereo. They huddled there like peas in a pod. So close, talking so much about who knows what.

And then I think about the Tatum twins wearing those outrageous boots they bought at the Salvation Army, boots that went up to the middle of their thick thighs, and I think about how they were dancing on the coffee table and how Bitsy knocked over six empty wine glasses and didn't break a single one.

Boy that was a good party.

I head upstairs to the bedroom carrying my cigarettes and my coffee mug. I want to tell Grace that that was a great party. That that was one hell of a good party. I want to tell Grace that we should have a party like that every night.

But then that tune Grace hummed in the kitchen jumps into my head and, instantly, I remember where I've heard it. I remember putting that very record on the stereo last night and watching it spin around and around. And then I think about how, when I went to put that record on, Bob and Grace stopped talking and just stared at me. They stopped their conversation, looked up and just stared. They both looked a little afraid of me, like I was going to punch them or something.

I stop on the stairs. I shake my head back and forth to clear it.

And, as I continue climbing up the stairs, holding my mug and my cigarettes, my headache comes back. All I can think about now is how that party last night wasn't really that great after all.

Swinging High

She has caught her little finger in the screen door for the second time today and she is howling. I go to the door and release her.

"For God's sake," I say.

She screams louder and louder. Her yells echo over the neighbourhood.

"That's the second time today," I say.

"I told you to stop playing with the door," I say.

"When will you ever learn?" I say.

She snuffles, wipes her nose with the back of her hand and blinks her eyes.

"It hurts," she says.

"Well, of course it hurts. That's the second time with the same finger. Of course it hurts."

I'm being tight but somehow I feel she deserves no sympathy. It doesn't matter to me that she is merely a child. She should know better.

"Go wash your hands. There's grease on your pinkie."

She holds up her pinkie finger and begins to cry again.

"It's crushed," she cries. "It's crushed. It's crushed. It's crushed."

"Don't be silly." But I still check the finger to make sure. I wouldn't want her father to think I watched a child of his deform her finger. Especially since the crushed finger would remind him of his wife.

It isn't crushed. It's just dirty, but Teeny's going on like she has just seen a ghost. She's screaming and hollering.

"Shut up and go wash."

She slams the screen door behind her and clumps angrily into the house. I can hear her knocking around for awhile.

I am sitting on the porch swing eating ice cream. I'm eating the cheap kind of ice cream, solid vanilla, the stuff that tastes like cardboard. I would've preferred a different flavour, even chocolate, but Mr. Adams hasn't been shopping in over a week and there is nothing else in the freezer.

I've been sitting here, swinging and eating, for most of the afternoon. Even though the kid drives me crazy, I'm happy to be doing it. It sure as hell beats working anywhere else. Besides, there is always the chance that Mr. Adams might notice me when he gets home.

Some people would say that I should entertain Teeny, that if I kept her occupied she wouldn't get into trouble. My thoughts on the matter are entirely different.

Teeny comes back out of the house with clean hands.

"Pat?" She is looking coy, like she wants something.

"What?" I swing as high as I can and, when the swing comes back down, I admire the fake grass covering on the porch. It looks to me like that stuff they put down in football stadiums. I call it fake grass. I have been here almost two months and this covering still astonishes me. You can spill just about anything on it and it will evaporate in the heat of the day, leaving no mark at all.

"Can I have ice cream?" Teeny asks.

I consider the question.

"If you get it yourself."

Teeny goes back into the house, careful not to stick her pinkie anywhere close to the screen door.

It is hot this summer. It's hotter than hell. Sometimes Teeny's best friend, Joanne, cons her parents into taking the two of them to the pool, sometimes Teeny and I go to the shopping centre, but most of the time Teeny just hangs around here, pestering me. Although it's my job and it pays OK, I'm getting fed up with her and this heat. I'm beginning to look forward to the end of summer even if that means school.

I shift my weight on the swing and it creaks.

Teeny comes out of the house with some ice cream. She licks her spoon noisily and glares at me from behind the rim of the bowl. I know she wants to be on the swing too.

"Stop staring," I say. "It isn't polite."

Teeny sits down on the front step with her back to me. She is wearing a triangle halter-top and pink shorts. Through the skin stretched tight across her back I can see her rib cage and spinal cord. I sometimes feel like snapping that cord, cracking it in two.

Teeny looks at me like she knows what I'm thinking. I swear I can see goose bumps on her back.

"You're staring," she says.

"I'm older," I say. That's my set answer.

"You say that about everything," Teeny says.

"Yeah, well, I'm older so I can do that."

"See," Teeny says.

I look at my watch. It's only two-thirty. Mr. Adams won't be back until five. I shift again, and again the swing creaks.

"You're going to bust that swing," Teeny says. "You're going to land on the floor one day because you're so fat."

I'm too hot to move to smack her so I throw my spoon at that spinal cord. She moves just in time.

"Shut up, kid," I say. But I know she's right. I am fat. I'm sixteen years old, five foot five, and I weigh over one hundred and eighty-five pounds. I've weighed less in my life, at one time or another, but for the last two years I've been going up on the scale. Sometimes, when I catch myself in a mirror, it astonishes me that this is my body. I feel much lighter than I am.

"Least my name isn't Teeny," I say.

"That isn't my name," Teeny says. Her little face curls up in a vicious scowl. "I'm called Teeny only because I'm smaller than the rest."

I don't know who "the rest" are but Teeny sure is tiny. She is smaller than a five-year-old, I'd say. She has tiny arms and legs and a tiny little torso. Even her face is tiny. Tiny nose and eyes and tiny, tiny lips. She isn't a midget or anything, she's just small for her age.

"Yeah, well." I want to say something mean but I can't think of anything. It's just too darn hot.

"Least I'm not fat," she says.

I want to throw something else at her but I have nothing in my hand but the bowl.

"Teeny Tiny Tina."

Teeny jumps up from the steps and stomps into the house. She's been really sensitive this summer, ever since her mother died. Me, I'd be happy to get rid of my mom.

Sometimes I wonder what would happen if I married Mr. Adams. I wonder if I'd have to adopt Teeny as my own. My mother says we already look like a freak show now and I'm only the babysitter—imagine if she was my adopted kid. The fat lady and the midget.

Sometimes I think that my mother gave me my name because it rhymes with fat. It's like she knew I was going to be fat the minute she looked at me. Patty fatty. Fat Pat.

I'm sitting here, on the swing, thinking these thoughts, not paying much heed to the noises I hear coming from inside the house, when Teeny appears in the screen door with the egg beaters in her hand.

"I'm making a cake," she says.

I ignore her.

Then she locks the screen door and then locks the wooden one.

Teeny's locked herself in the house.

Half of me wants to be concerned. I want to cry out and pound on the door and worry about her burning the house down or stabbing herself with a knife. But that half of me just isn't there. Instead I can't help but wish Teeny would go to hell. It's too damn hot to play these games. Then I wish that Teeny really would make a cake and then I imagine her serving me a large slice of chocolate ribbon cake on a china plate with a silver fork. She's in a maid uniform and I'm slim and tanned.

I light a cigarette up while I think about the situation. I'm not allowed to smoke at home even though I half-persuaded my mother that it would help me lose weight. My father just wouldn't believe that. Mr. Adams doesn't mind, though. He smokes too. He just told me to smoke carefully. Just smoke with caution, he said.

I can hear noises from the kitchen coming through the screened front windows. Teeny's smashing things around and I hear the fridge opening and closing.

"Do you even know what's in a cake?" I holler into the house, without moving from the swing. I let the cigarette dangle from my lips like I've seen them do in the movies.

"Flour, sugar, eggs . . ." Teeny starts a list that makes me hungry. When she gets to chocolate my stomach rumbles.

"Do you know how to turn the oven on?" I shout.

"I'm not fat Pat like you," she screams back. I have no idea what that means.

I wonder what kind of a mess the house will be in when I finally get enough energy up to go inside. I wonder who taught Teeny how to make a cake. I wonder if Mr. Adams ever cooks. I can imagine Mr. Adams in an apron, tossing an omelet, frying a steak. I imagine him bringing food to me in bed. I'm wearing a thin negligee, purple perhaps, and my hair is long and shiny. I'm slender. Slender, not skinny. I imagine Mr. Adams tripping slightly (because he is stunned at my beauty) and spilling the food all over me. And then I think about him climbing into bed to kiss all the spilt food off—

"Where's the oatmeal?" Teeny shouts.

"You have to come out here to ask me questions." I think I can probably grab her if she's dumb enough to unlock the door.

"I'm not coming out," Teeny says. "I'll just use Special K."

I get back into my daydream just in time to see Mr. Adams take off his shirt.

"Where's the molasses?" Teeny is beginning to get on my nerves. "What do you do if there's fire?"

"Teeny, enough's enough. Open the door." I pull myself off the swing and hobble stiffly over to the door. I've been sitting so long I have lines on my legs. I pull my shorts legs down and adjust my T-shirt. "Let me in!"

I peek through the front screened window, right beside the door. I can see Teeny in the kitchen, standing on a chair, stirring something with the egg beaters. She keeps looking nervously towards the stove.

"Let me in, you jerk," I say. "I'll tell your father."

Teeny just looks over, towards my voice. Her tiny little hands keep stirring with the egg beater.

I can see that all the burners on the stove are on. The red-hot coils are glowing.

"What do you have the burners on for?"

"For the cake," Teeny says.

"Those are for frying, you jerk." Teeny is getting on my nerves. And it's so damn hot. My cigarette is all finished so I throw it down and begin to pound on the door.

"You open up this door this minute!" I sound like my mother.

"No!" Teeny is annoyingly stubborn.

I pound some more. As I'm pounding I decide that I'll never have kids. I think I'll marry Mr. Adams and then ship Teeny off to a private school in the Yukon. I once read about this school up there that is just like the military. The girls have to jog and do exercises every morning and they only get oatmeal for breakfast. Or porridge. It will only be a matter of time before Mr. Adams stops mourning his wife. My mother says that men forget about women as soon as they aren't there.

When I think about Mrs. Adams I get these creepy feelings. She was small too, come to think of it. Just like Teeny. She was tiny and beautiful and really thin. She was always playing tennis and she taught at the elementary school. It's amazing to me that one day you can be healthy and happy, having a barbecue, all your friends in the back yard, your kid rushing around in the sprinkler, and the very next day you can get hit by a car, get your skull crushed, and be lying dead in a closed coffin. It's amazing to me. The whole thing just blows me away.

But that's more reason for Mr. Adams to marry me. He needs someone to comfort him. Someone soft and large, like me, to hold him tight.

I bet if I got hit by a car I'd bounce right off. That's one good thing about being fat—you're more durable. I should tell my mother that one.

"Teeny, let me in." I can smell something cooking, or burning. It's a pretty powerful smell. Kind of like plastic. Not at all like a cake. All I can think about is: if the house burns down, will Mr. Adams still pay me for the week?

All of a sudden the front door bursts open and Teeny stands there, looking mighty proud.

"Look," she says and she produces some sticky-looking batter in a cake pan. I can still smell the burning smell but it's not coming from inside the house.

"Look," she says again and this time Teeny is pointing, wide-eyed, to the porch floor.

I look down and, oh my God, my cigarette has set the porch on fire. This fake-grass stuff burns in a peculiar manner. It really just disappears, you can't see any flames. The edges get dark and then part of the grass just vanishes. Right now I'm looking at a hole about the size of a watermelon.

"Oh my God."

Teeny and I start stamping around on the hole and on the outer edges of the hole with our running shoes. We are hollering. She is still holding the cake pan and, with her tiny little body and her jerky movements, she reminds me of one of those pygmies I saw on late-night TV. We keep stamping but one corner of the hole just seems to be getting bigger and bigger no matter how hard we jump. We jump into each other and pound our feet down upon the large hole. And then, suddenly, Teeny's little face lights up and she tosses the cake pan on top of the fire.

She turns it over with skill and dumps the gooey mixture all over the widening hole.

"There," she says. The fire's out.

We are breathless. We are exhausted. It is so damn hot and the porch is a mess and I'm feeling faint. But Teeny's looking great. Her face is bright and her cheeks are red. She is panting. She is covered with cake stuff—flour and sugar. There is a Special K piece in her hair. But she looks great. She looks really happy, really excited.

"Mom taught me that," she says. She points to the cake batter on the hole on the porch floor.

"What?" I have no idea what she is talking about.

"Mom taught me to dump baking soda on fires to put them out. Cake has baking soda in it." This is the first time I've heard Teeny mention her mother without crying.

"Oh," I say.

"That's great," she says.

"What's great?"

"That I remember," she says. "That I remember all this stuff."

I just look at her. Teeny suddenly looks larger than she really is. I guess it's just because she's happy.

I wonder if I would look thinner if I was happy. My mother always tells me to change my outlook on life. I sit down on the porch swing, thinking about this.

"Don't play with matches, never talk to strangers, don't take candy from strangers except at Halloween—"

Teeny is rambling on and on and on. She sits down next to me on the swing, counting things off on her fingers.

"Don't put your finger in holes in the ground, don't go swimming right after you've eaten—"

I listen to Teeny babble. She is flushed and her eyes are shining. She has counted all her fingers and now she's working on her toes. I begin to swing her high into the air and she laughs when the breeze hits her face. I hold up my fingers and she counts those.

"If you smile people will like you, wash your hands after you read the newspaper—"

I'm wondering when Teeny has ever read the newspaper and then I realize that Mrs. Adams must have said that to Mr. Adams.

"If you smell gas in the house get out immediately—"

Teeny starts to giggle when I pull the Special K piece out of her hair. She giggles so hard I think she's going to faint. I give her the Special K flake and she eats it. This is just about the funniest thing in the world to Teeny.

You know, this kid's not all that bad. She's got a great sense of humour and she really knows how to laugh.

Look at us. The fat lady and the tiny, tiny girl swinging high on the porch swing. The fake grass by the front door is a mess, the kitchen is a disaster, it's the hottest summer on record and we've destroyed the house—but look at us, Teeny and me, swinging on the porch swing, laughing. Tomorrow, if I'm still employed here, I think we'll go to the pool. Maybe we'll call Joanne and walk to the pool. Maybe I'll even use my savings to buy them ice cream.

A chocolate fudge ripple cone with strawberry and grape sprinkles. Or maybe a neon-opolitan cone or hazelnut or a white chocolate chunks cone or the cookie batter type.

There are so many wonderful flavours of ice cream to choose from in this world.

The Diner

"She says she hopes we are well," Bella calls to Ranger as she climbs into the car.

"And what did you say?"

"I said we were fine, just fine."

Ranger rolls up his window and starts the engine. Bella fastens her seatbelt and smooths down her skirt. Driving away from the phone booth, Bella glances behind her, out the back window, and imagines she sees something in the dust from the car.

"Funny, isn't it?"

"What's funny?" Ranger looks over at Bella. He senses something in her voice. "What's funny?" he says again.

"The phone booth."

"Why?"

"Well, it's just there. Just there in the country with nothing else around it."

"Lucky for us, though," says Ranger. He watches the bends in the road while he taps his fingers on the steering wheel.

"I wonder who fixes it if it breaks," Bella says.

Ranger shrugs.

"I just wonder, that's all." Bella opens her window and dangles her hand out. She flops her hand up and down in the stiff breeze. She pats the air. "Pat, pat," she whispers.

"What else did she say?" Ranger asks.

"Hmm?" Bella pats a bird resting delicately in a sumac bush.

"What else did Martha say on the phone?"

"Oh, all sorts of things." She pats the clouds and then puts her thumb and middle finger together and pings the sun.

"Like what?"

"Well, she asked about Davie."

"Did you tell her?" Ranger's voice tightens and he glances quickly in Bella's direction.

"How could I, Ranger? I mean, really, how could I?"

"Well, I think you should have told her," Ranger says.

"On the phone?" Bella stops patting things and looks at the side of Ranger's face. He didn't shave this morning. She pats his stubble.

"I'm driving," Ranger says.

"Now, don't be mad." She brings her hands down to her lap. "I couldn't tell her on the phone, Ranger. It wouldn't have been fair. I'll tell her tonight, when we get there."

"I think you should have told her last month when it happened."

"I know what you think, Ranger."

Ranger grunts and then bends slowly towards the radio, keeping his eyes on the road. "Wonder if I can get any stations out here."

"Let me try. You're driving." Bella pushes Ranger away and then fiddles with the dials. All she comes up with is a choking static that makes her want to cry.

"Why did you mention Davie?" she blurts out.

"You mentioned him, Bella. You brought him up first."

"Well, I just thought we were on holiday, that's all."

"I didn't mention him."

"I thought we weren't going to talk about him. I thought we were going to enjoy ourselves, forget everything, not mention him for awhile."

Ranger looks quickly at Bella. She is hunched down in the passenger seat, rooting through her purse.

"What are you looking for, honey?"

"A Kleenex," Bella says. "I need a Kleenex to blow my nose."

Ranger inspects the road ahead of him. He clears his throat. "Look up there," he says. "A diner."

Bella looks up from her purse. She sees the diner, a small, squat building surrounded by several scrawny trees. A neon sign flickers on and off but Bella can't read it without her glasses. Bella turns towards Ranger and pulls at the wheel. "Stop, Ranger! Stop!" Her voice is frantic.

Ranger swerves the car quickly into the parking lot of the diner and then slams on the brakes.

"What the hell?"

"I wasn't sure you'd stop in time. I thought you'd drive right past like you did with the last diner." Bella gets out of the car and adjusts her dress. "My, I'm wrinkled," she says to no one in particular.

Ranger sits in the car for a moment, collecting his thoughts and catching his breath. After a second or two he reaches into the back seat and grabs his hat. He gets out of the car and follows Bella into the diner.

The diner is air-conditioned and Bella shivers a little as she looks at the menu.

"What are you having, Ranger?"

Ranger glances down at the menu and then up at Bella. He notices that her lipstick has bled outside of her lips and the effect is off-putting.

"Don't know," he says.

"Well, the egg salad looks good. Or the tuna sandwich maybe."

"Why don't you just decide for yourself, Bella, and I'll figure out what I want to eat."

"My!" Bella says and then smiles. She puts down her menu and looks up at Ranger. "My, you're getting snippy."

"You almost killed us out there," Ranger says and flicks his thumb towards their car, parked at an angle just outside the window. He feels like hissing at her. Instead he whispers deeply, "That was really irresponsible."

"My, my, my," Bella says. She looks long and hard at Ranger and then picks up her menu again. "I'm having the egg salad with chips, I think."

The waitress sidles over to their table with a coffee pot in her hand.

"What can I get you folks?" She has on a red name tag with "Bessy" embroidered in white.

Bella smiles up at the waitress. "I'll have the tuna sandwich with chips," she says. Her bleeding lipstick makes her smile large and unnatural.

"I thought you were getting the egg salad."

"I changed my mind." Bella flashes Ranger a lopsided smile. Bessy writes down Bella's order.

"And you?"

"I'll have the same," Ranger says. "And coffee."

Bessy pours coffee for both of them and then moves away from their table and into the kitchen.

"Just like the movies, isn't it?"

"What are you talking about now?" Ranger sips at his coffee and then adds sugar.

"The diner. Just like the movies," Bella says.

"Aren't you going to use the washroom?" Ranger asks. He is hoping that she'll wipe that lipstick off her face.

"Good idea." Bella gets up from the bench and walks over to Bessy who is standing behind the counter.

Ranger watches her walk away and then he looks into the space of the restaurant. There is a surprisingly large number of people in the diner. They are quietly eating, sitting in stiff, burgundy benches under the tinted, dirty windows. Ranger thinks it is strange that so many people are in the restaurant when his is the only car in the parking lot. He peers out the window to see if there are any houses nearby, but from his vantage point, all he can see is the country road and then the fields and the hills and the trees.

Bella is in the washroom redoing her lipstick. She can't believe Ranger didn't tell her it was smeared all over her face. Bella brushes back her hair with her hands and applies the lipstick. She pushes the water tap on and washes her hands. "Why ever did I get tuna?" she says to her reflection. "I really wanted egg salad."

When Bella gets back to the table her sandwich is there and her coffee has been topped up. Although Ranger has had a chip or two, he is waiting for Bella before he eats.

"Go ahead, eat," Bella says. She slides herself onto the bench. "Why didn't you tell me about my lipstick, Ranger?"

"What?" Ranger's mouth is full of tuna sandwich.

"My lipstick was all over my face. Why didn't you tell me?" Bella picks up a chip and crunches it loudly.

"Didn't notice." Ranger is eating quickly. He didn't realize how hungry he was until he began to eat.

Bella picks at her sandwich.

"Ranger," she says. "I've been thinking that perhaps we shouldn't be doing this right now."

Ranger stops chewing and looks closely at Bella. He is trying to figure out what she is talking about.

"I've been thinking that my sister doesn't really need us bothering her right now. She's got enough to worry about—what with Ernie losing his job and Maggie breaking her big toe—"

"Stop right there." Ranger holds a potato chip up in the air and points it threateningly at Bella. "Just stop what you're saying, Bella. Stop right there."

Bella picks up her tuna sandwich and takes a large bite. It is better than she thought it would be.

"Don't get angry, Ranger. Don't get all put out."

"Put out?" Ranger eats the potato chip and then throws his hands up in the air. "For Christ's sake, Bella."

"Now don't you start swearing, Ranger."

The waitress moves over to their table. "More coffee?"

"Yes, lovely," Bella smiles. "Thank you."

Ranger grunts and finishes his sandwich. Bessy fills up their cups and moves away.

"I just don't know if I want to see her right now. I don't know if I can deal with it right now, Ranger. Don't you see?"

"I'm not one to say I told you so . . . ," Ranger starts. Then he pauses, sighs and wipes his mouth with a napkin. "Bella, I didn't want to come in the first place. You know that."

"I can't possibly tell her about Davie," Bella whispers, almost to herself. She isn't listening to Ranger. "How do you tell someone something like that? How? I don't know." Bella sighs. "I don't know how to tell her Davie is dead." Bella looks up.

Ranger looks as if he might cry, and when Bella sees that, she can't swallow her bite. Her throat has closed up and her mouth is dry. The tuna smells and Bella feels suddenly very, very ill.

"Why didn't you tell her before? Why?" Ranger speaks slowly and carefully. "How could you not tell her?" He rubs his eyes.

Bella spits the piece of tuna sandwich out onto her plate. She looks at the half-chewed piece for a second. She pokes it with her fork. Then she puts her fork down slowly and rushes out of the diner. All of the people in the diner stop eating and stare at Bella as she runs towards the only car in the parking lot. Ranger pays the bill. He can see Bella leaning up against their large, blue car. Her whole body is shaking as she rummages through her purse, looking for a Kleenex.

Ranger shifts in his seat and then glances quickly at Bella.

"Are you ready to talk now?" He is almost whispering.

"What?"

"I said, are you ready to talk now?"

"Oh, Ranger, I don't know." Bella wipes her nose on a Kleenex. "You sound just like Dr. Ross."

"Yes, I guess I do." Ranger looks back at the road. They have been driving for at least an hour since the diner and Ranger still hasn't seen any houses. He can't stop wondering how all those people got to the diner. But then he thinks that maybe they were on a bus trip and the bus left to get gas while the people were eating their lunch. Ranger tosses this idea back and forth in his mind until he realizes that that really wouldn't make any sense. He realizes that no one in the restaurant even acted like they knew one another. Ranger has heard that on bus trips everyone becomes really friendly.

"Well, I'm ready now," Bella says.

"Ready for what?" Ranger is off track, he has forgotten what they are talking about.

"Ready to talk, Dr. Ross." Bella laughs. Her laugh hangs in the air. Ranger rolls down his window and lets it out.

"Don't call me that. I'm nothing like him."

"You've picked things up, though." Bella rolls down her window too and the air swishes around the car, making it difficult to talk.

"Like what?" Ranger shouts.

"Like the way you say, 'Are you ready to talk now?' Things like that."

"Humph." Ranger can't think of anything to say. The wind is whistling through his ears and the country on either side of the car is darkening with shadow.

Still no houses or buildings.

"Looks like rain," Bella says.

"Maybe if I'd been more like him Davie wouldn't be dead," Ranger says.

"Like who?"

"Dr. Ross."

Bella looks closely at Ranger's face. He has a large, square face and his jaw is tilted at a cocky angle. His face is wide and innocent and beautiful. Bella sniffs.

"Don't be silly, Ranger. We didn't do anything wrong."

"Now you're sounding like Dr. Ross."

Bella and Ranger look at each other and laugh. Ranger reaches out and pats Bella's leg.

"Look, another diner," Bella shouts.

"Oh no you don't." Ranger pushes Bella's hand away from the steering wheel and they pass the diner in a cloud of dust.

Bella and Ranger approach Martha's street. It is dusk and the streetlights flicker on.

"How will I tell her?" Bella asks.

"You'll know when you see her."

"But how will she react? Won't she blame us? Won't she be angry that we didn't tell her at the time?"

"Bella . . . breathe."

The windows are up in the car and Bella and Ranger are whispering. The street they are driving on is tree-lined and quiet. Bella can see a family of four sitting down for dinner in their brightly lit dining area.

"Maybe I don't have to tell her, Ranger," she says. "Maybe she won't ask about him. Maybe . . ."

"Bella."

"Ranger, maybe they will never have to know. I mean, maybe they will never ask and maybe I'll never have to tell them."

Ranger grunts. "Which house is it again?"

"It just hurts so much to know," Bella says. "I'd rather they didn't know."

They pull the car into the driveway and Bella gets out slowly and deliberately. She gets out of the car, straightens her skirt and breathes deeply. The air is refreshing and cool. Bella looks around at the open spaces surrounding her, the large, tree-lined, peaceful spaces, and she breathes again.

Ranger imagines the people in the diner walking over fields and through streams. Walking towards the diner for their lunch. Ordering tuna or egg salad. He imagines them, moving quietly and slowly, walking with only one purpose in mind. A stream of people flowing over a field, coming from nowhere. Ranger sighs.

And then Martha comes slowly out of the house, drying her hands on a dish towel, and Bella looks at her and then looks up at the wide, darkening sky.

Ranger watches them as they approach each other. He watches Bella's body relax and Martha's smile grow wider.

"How was the drive, you two?" Martha calls out sweetly as she comes closer.

"Fine," Bella says and steps out of the open space and into Martha's warm, comforting arms. "Everything is fine, Martha. Just fine."

Bug Shields
and Gun Racks

*B*en drives up in his old truck and the first thing I notice is the new bug shield. He's had a gun rack, black dice and a handicap parking sticker for some time now but the bug shield is new. So new it shines.

"There are no bugs on your shield yet, Ben," I say after he has climbed down from the truck and walked over to me.

"There'll soon be." Ben fires his answer at me like a bark. His radio in the truck must have been turned loud because Ben is shouting like he has just walked out of a rock concert.

"Yes," I say quietly, "there will soon be plenty of bugs." Ben looks up into the sky as if he expects a plague of locusts to fall. Then he sits down next to me and pulls out a package of gum. He offers me a stick.

"No thanks," I say. I light up a cigarette. We sit silently chewing and smoking.

We are sitting on a bench in front of Della's Hardware store at the corner of Main and Mckenzie. It's Monday. We do this most afternoons, watch the customers come and go and nod at people we know. Like Rita, from the bank.

"Hey, Rita!" Ben spits out in staccato.

"Hey, hot stuff," Rita says. She waves at us and waddles into the hardware store. Ben and I look at each other. I don't know which one of us she is talking about, which one of us is hot in her estimation. We look back out at the street and I scratch the stubble on my chin. Ben coughs. Rita is friends with Della and they sit in the back office every afternoon drinking coffee and smoking American cigarettes.

"Christine's late today," Ben says, chewing his gum hard.

"Don't fret, she'll be here." Ben has this thing about Christine Pillar. She comes in most every afternoon to buy glue sticks for her grade one class. It used to bother me to no end that a bunch of kids could go through so much glue in a week. But now it seems commonplace. I guess things seem common once you become used to them.

"This bug shield is from Toronto," Ben says. He points over to his truck as if I had forgotten what a bug shield was, as if I hadn't been laid off last year from Dale's Auto Shop. "I was visiting Virgil this weekend and I bought it at the Canadian Tire store."

"No kidding."

"Yeah. They got so much selection there it's unreal." Ben grinds down on his gum and I can hear his teeth clack together. "They got a whole section just for different types of garden hoses."

"Who'd believe that," I say.

"Yeah." Ben looks over at his truck.

"Well, you sure picked a nice one," I say.

"Yeah. Had my choice too." Ben scratches around in his hair for awhile. "I had a choice between colours even. Imagine a blue bug shield!" Ben lets out a short laugh.

I laugh. "Funny how some people will buy anything just to draw attention to themselves," I say.

Ben nods. Just then Christine Pillar comes around the corner and heads straight for Della's Hardware. Rita is coming out the front door and I can see a collision in the making. Christine is looking at Ben and Rita is waving back into the store at Della and suddenly everything goes in slow motion and the door smacks Christine hard on the forehead and Rita falls out into the street.

"Holy shit," Ben says, under his breath.

Rita is lying half on the sidewalk and half on the curb. She has a cut on her chin and her left arm looks twisted and funny. Christine is sitting up on the sidewalk with her legs straight out in front of her. It looks to me like her forehead has flattened right in. It looks like she's got one awful dent on that forehead.

"Are you all right?" Ben is helping Christine stand. When Ben touches her she turns red and moves her head around nervously.

"My arm!" Rita has pulled herself out of the road and is now lying mostly on the sidewalk. "Oh God, my arm," she roars.

Della comes running out of her store. Andy Fowl, who happens to be walking past, stops to help out. We work together to lift Rita onto the bench Ben and I were just sitting on.

Christine comes right over, dented forehead and all, and immediately apologizes, taking all the blame.

"No, honey, I wasn't looking either," Rita says, and both women shush each other and pat each other's sore parts. Rita has managed to untwist her arm and now she thinks she can make it up to Doctor Randall's office on her own.

"It's just right there. It'll be no problem." Rita points towards the Health Clinic as if we all haven't been living in Fraser Point for our entire lives. Ben keeps offering her a ride in his truck, but, as Rita points out, climbing up into that thing would most likely lead to another accident.

So Rita waddles up the street clutching at her arm, Christine rubs her head and goes into Della's to buy glue, and Andy Fowl nods at Ben and me and then walks towards the barber shop. Ben and I sit back down on the bench. I light up another cigarette and Ben pulls out his pack of gum.

We are silent for awhile as we collect our thoughts.

"So Canadian Tire is large, eh?" I ask.

"Oh yeah. It's huge." We look at Ben's truck and admire his bug shield. Christine comes out of the store with her package of glue and moves nervously over to our bench.

"More glue?" I ask, to be polite.

"Yeah. You would think that some of the kids were eating it or something," Christine says and then she giggles. Ben stares stupidly at her but he doesn't say anything. "Thanks for helping me up, Ben." She says this so quietly I can barely hear her. Ben nods at her and I notice his mouth is hanging open.

"Bye now." Christine stands there, hugging her package to her chest. Then she turns and walks down the street in the direction of the school.

Ben watches her walk away and then he says, "Four o'clock."

"Already?" I look at my watch. "Well, I'll have cherry this time."

Ben nods and then walks over to his truck and climbs in. He starts the motor, backs up and then drives down the street a bit. He pulls up in front of The Delectable Bakery. If I squint I can see him through the windows, pointing out what he wants and filling a couple of styrofoam cups with coffee. Then he climbs back in his truck, spins the wheels turning, and drives back to Della's Hardware.

Once settled on the bench again Ben hands me a paper bag and my cup of coffee.

"Didn't have cherry today," he says.

"Damn." I open the bag and take out a lemon Danish. "So, what's Virgil been up to these days?"

Ben has his mouth full with cinnamon twist. He just looks at me while he mouths the bite around a bit and then swallows.

"Unemployed," he manages to get out.

"Oh," I say. "Again?"

"Yeah. Virgil hasn't had steady work in about a year. Bad times." Ben stuffs the rest of the twist in his mouth and then gulps back some black coffee.

Della comes out of the store.

"Hey there." She sits down next to Ben.

"Hey to you too," I say. Della smiles.

"How's business?" Ben asks.

"Oh, you know," Della sighs, "could be better, could be worse."

"Yeah."

We all stare at Ben's truck.

"What about you two? What are you two up to these days?"

"Same as always," I say. "Nothing ever changes."

"Yeah, I know." Della nods her head up and down rapidly. She has large curls and with each nod her curls bounce higher and higher. I think she nods so much just for the effect. "My son's in Ottawa, in school," she says. "Got himself a job with the government. A bit of money to help to pay for his schooling."

"Yeah?" Ben and I know this. She tells us this every day but we use her bench so we think we should be polite.

"He's a parliamentary aide," she says. "He takes messages to the politicians."

"That so," I say. I've seen him on TV. He wears this outfit and he rushes about looking busy.

"Things are tough all over but Richard got himself a good job in Ottawa."

"Yeah." Ben is silent. I don't really know what to say to all of that.

"I wonder how Rita is," Della says. "Have you seen her leave the clinic yet?"

"No. I haven't seen her at all," Ben says. Ben looks at me with his eyebrows raised. "You see her when I went to the bakery?"

"Nope," I say. "Haven't seen her leave yet."

"Well, you tell me if you see her before you leave," Della says. She nods her head again a couple of times and then she walks back into the store. Just when the door shuts behind her I see Rita leave the doctor's office. She has a cast on her arm and she's carrying a large yellow envelope.

"Must be her X-rays," Ben says, indicating the envelope.

"Yeah, I guess. You wanna tell Della?"

"No, you do it. I got the donuts."

So I unstick myself from the bench, hike up my jeans and poke my head through Della's store. It is dim and hot in there and it smells like American cigarettes.

"Rita's out of the doctor's," I say. "She's headed home, it looks like."

"Thanks." Della pokes her head around from the cash register and nods at me. Her curls shoot out in all directions. "I'll call her in a bit to make sure she's fine."

Back at the bench Ben is talking to Mr. Rainsford.

"Any luck hunting this season?" Rainsford asks.

"No. Haven't really been much." Ben stares at his feet.

"Well, you ought to get out there, son," Rainsford says. "Truck like yours could get you right into deep bush to hunt." He points towards Ben's truck. Ben looks at Mr. Rainsford's pointing finger. "And it would get you home safely too."

"Yes, I suppose it would." Ben stares at his truck. Mr. Rainsford walks into Della's.

"Afternoon," he says as he passes me.

"That's an idea," I say to Ben. "Let's go hunting tomorrow."

Ben looks at me. "What about Christine?"

"What about her?"

Ben just stares.

"Aw shit, Ben. You can see her on Wednesday. You can miss one day, can't you?"

"Yeah." Ben looks back at his truck. "Be a good opportunity to test out that bug shield," he says. "Be a good time to see if I need to take it back or something."

"What could be wrong with it?"

"I don't know. Anything, I guess. I could take it back on the weekend and stay at Virgil's. I could see that Canadian Tire store again."

"Yeah," I say.

"Maybe you could come along and see the store."

I nod. "So what do you say about hunting tomorrow?"

"Hunting would be good," Ben says. "I'll just clip on the guns and pick you up at six."

"Yeah, fine."

It is five o'clock now. We sit there, in front of Della's Hardware store, and watch the people leave their jobs and close up the stores. I'm stiff when I get up to go home. I can feel marks from the bench on the backs of my legs. I'm thinking about how it's almost like I've been glued there. Then I think about Christine.

"See you tomorrow, Ben," I say to remind him that we are going hunting.

"Yeah," Ben says. "Six sharp. We'll make sure that bug shield works."

I walk home alone as the sun gradually sets and the street-lights come on. As I pass the school I can see Christine in her classroom sitting at her desk with her head in her hands. She is rocking in her chair. Her head is in her hands and all those glue sticks are piled up around her. I don't know much about teaching grade one, but it seems to me that she has way too many glue sticks around her. I swear I can see hundreds of them, yellow with black writing and white caps.

After I've been staring for a few minutes Christine looks up at me and waves. I can see a large purple and black bruise surrounding the dent on her forehead. I wave back and then turn to head home. As I walk home I think about how much I'm looking forward to hunting tomorrow. Then I think about Christine and Ben and I wonder if Ben knows how Christine feels about him.

On Chestnut Road Mr. Dickson is outside cutting his grass. I can see Mrs. Dickson drinking a can of Coke on the patio. I wave. As I turn from Chestnut onto Woodley my thoughts turn once again to hunting and I wonder if Ben will really pick me up tomorrow. I think about how I haven't been out of Fraser Point in a long time and, even if we go only as far as Drake's Woods, it will still feel like I'm going somewhere a long way away.

Orange Cowboy Boots

Susan's mother wants to buy a pair of bright orange cowboy boots. She has been talking about it for weeks. They are at Boots N'Gals in the Eaton Centre and Susan's mother is standing next to the cowboy boot display. She is resting her thick hands on her huge hips. She is panting and her forehead is shiny. Her bulky purse is falling off one shoulder and she is shaking her massive head back and forth.

"Whatever happened to good, old-fashioned, bright orange cowboy boots?" she asks loudly.

Susan shrugs and looks around at the people staring at them.

"I mean, look at this." Susan's mother holds up a pair of turquoise, fake-snakeskin boots and thrusts them in Susan's face. "Look at this! It's fake. It isn't even snakeskin. And the dye would probably run if you wore them in the rain. You'd have blue socks, Susan. And blue toes, too."

Susan nods. Her naturally pink face turns a deeper pink. She can't stop looking around, watching the people who are watching them.

"Look here, Susan. There's red and turquoise and black and brown and even yellow. But, I ask you, where the hell is the orange? That's all I want. That's all I came here for." She gestures over her shoulder, back towards the large mall, towards the glass ceiling and the wooden wild Canadian geese hanging stiffly by wire. "That's all I ask," she says. "A pair of size eleven bright orange cowboy boots." She sighs. "With pointy, pointy toes."

Susan looks out of the Boots N'Gals store, towards where her mother is gesturing. She sees a crowd of girls her age backing noisily into the Fairweather store. They are laughing and pointing at a group of boys. The boys are lounging on the benches adjacent to Boots N'Gals. Susan looks quickly back to her mother.

"Well, I never." Susan's mother picks up a pair of boots with square toes. She scratches her head and Susan can see flakes of dandruff fall onto her neon green T-shirt. The boots she is holding are pink and studded with gemstones. She holds them up to the lights and the stones twinkle. "Imagine wearing these," she says. "Just imagine."

Susan quietly leaves her mother's side and wanders to the back of the store. She picks up a pair of men's work boots. She holds them up to the light and rubs at them with her red and black plaid, flannel, hand-me-down jacket. She smooths the leather with her hands and taps at the steel toe. Even though it is Saturday it is deserted and quiet at the back of the store. The customers are milling about up front where the boots are on sale. Susan pulls the tongue out of one of the work boots and looks inside. There is red flannel inside and Susan can't help but think that this boot looks comfortable and solid. A good buy, she thinks. Susan pushes her nose into the boot and sniffs deeply.

"Get a load of these." Susan's mother comes barrelling down the aisle carrying a pair of zebra-striped boots. Her body sways back and forth as she moves towards Susan. She blocks out all the light from the front of the store and Susan imagines she can feel the floor shake. "Get your nose out of those boots,

Susan! You don't know where they've been! You don't know what kind of people have tried them on!"

Susan takes her nose out of the boot and looks at her mother. Then she looks down at the floor. The red carpet becomes a blur and the sounds of the mall creep up and penetrate her ears. She rubs her head, pushing a nasty headache away.

"Look at these." Susan's mother holds up the zebra-striped boots and then lets out a small whoop. "Get a load of these," she laughs loudly. A salesperson passes and smiles in amazement at Susan's mother. She smiles back.

"Are we finished here yet?"

"What do you mean?" Susan's mother glances at her.

"Can we go now? Are we finished yet?"

"Does it look like we're finished, Susan?" She holds up her hands. "We have only just begun. I haven't even tried any on yet. I haven't even bought the boots I wanted to buy."

"But there aren't any orange ones here," Susan says.

"How do you know that, Susan? Have you asked the salesperson, have you spoken to the manager? How do you know there aren't any orange boots in the back of the store?"

Susan sits down on a burgundy, vinyl-covered bench.

"What's your problem today, anyway? What's wrong with you, Miss Grumpy? Got your period?" she laughs and Susan feels herself sinking into the bench. She shrugs her shoulders at her mother and then slumps into a more comfortable position.

"Sit straight, honey. We'll get boots sooner than you know it. Then we can go for lunch." Susan's mother sways back down the aisle towards the front of the store. "We can go for pizza or something," she calls back. Susan watches the large hips roll and the meaty thighs rub together as her mother walks quickly after a sales person. She is talking to him before she has even reached him. Her voice is loud and friendly. "I'm looking for orange cowboy boots with pointy toes. Size eleven or even twelve, depending on the width."

They leave the store half an hour later. Susan's mother carries her boot bag by a string. She swings it back and forth, occasionally knocking it into her large legs. She breathes heavily and breaks out into a sweat. Her enormous chest bounces up and down to the rhythm of her pace.

"I just had to buy them, didn't I? I didn't want that colour but they just made my feet look so tiny—"

Susan nods.

"I can't believe you can't get orange boots anywhere in this city. I can't believe it. You'd think we were in some small town, wouldn't you? I can't believe it."

Susan stares straight ahead and walks quickly. Her mother is slightly behind her and she is panting loudly.

"Where should we go for lunch? Buying boots is a reason to celebrate. I should have worn them home. I should stop right here and put them on, shouldn't I? Wait up, Susan."

Susan stops, turns and pulls at her mother's arm. "Let's just go, OK?"

"No, wait. Stop. I'm putting them on right here. Just hold up a minute."

Susan's mother groans as she bends down and settles herself onto a stone bench in front of a fountain. She places her purse beside her and her boot bag on her lap.

"Undo my shoes, will you honey?"

Susan looks around. She feels panicky. The mall suddenly feels very large and, at the same time, very small. Susan's hands move up to her head, instinctively pushing away the shrinking walls.

"No," Susan whispers. The whisper exits her mouth like a hiss. It is pushed out through tight lips.

"What?" Susan's mother isn't paying any attention. She is trying to touch her own feet. She is groaning. Her arms don't reach over the layers of chest and fat and muscle. "Take them off, Susan, and then I'll wear my boots home."

"No." Susan looks around. She sees the group of Fairweather girls in the glass elevators with the boys who were lounging on the benches. One girl is putting on her lipstick, and when she is finished, she kisses the glass wall of the elevator. She looks right at Susan and kisses the glass wall of the elevator. The elevator stops and the girls all pile out. They are laughing and stumbling. Their bodies are smooth and sleek. Susan watches their hips sway, their long legs moving to some quiet rhythm. She watches their breasts, small and pointy, poking out from tight t-shirts. The boys follow, staying far enough back to take everything in. Susan looks back at the elevator and sees that lone kiss hanging in mid-air over the Eaton Centre.

"What did you say? What are you saying?"

"I won't take your shoes off for you here. I won't do it."

"Oh." Susan's mother leans back against the stone. She looks up at her daughter and then to the group of girls being followed by the boys. "Oh," she says again. She suddenly feels very tired and slightly sick. Her legs ache and her heart won't stop beating wildly. She can feel it in her lungs. She realizes she is still panting. She looks down at her boots, so very far away, and she shakes her head.

Susan sits down beside her mother. "Can we go? Can't we just go now?"

"All I wanted was orange cowboy boots, Susan. That's all I wanted." Susan's mother pulls herself up from her sitting position and stands a few feet away. Susan's shoulders slump forward as she sits on the stone bench and watches the floor of the mall. She watches all the shoes going past. She sits there and watches until soon all the other movement in the mall takes over. She looks up and sees the people moving all around her. It is Saturday and it is crowded. Susan watches until, out of the corner of her eye, she notices the Fairweather lipstick girl trying on a striped midriff in Reitman's. Her stomach is bare and lean and pale. She turns around and around in front of the full-length mirror, admiring every inch of her own body. There is a dark mole directly above her navel. She is so skinny that Susan can see the bottom of her ribs poking out of the midriff like a second set of breasts.

"Do you want to go home now?" Susan's mother's voice comes out of nowhere. "I mean, I've got the boots, I'm happy."

You're obviously not, though." She fumbles with her words. "I could go home or I could go out for lunch. Either is all right with me, Susan. You choose. Pizza would be good. Or maybe a hamburger." Her stomach growls.

Susan stands up. She looks at her mother's huge, awkward body.

"Let's go for lunch," Susan says quietly.

As they walk away Susan's mother looks down and notices something. Her heart speeds up and she smiles widely. "Look, Susan," she says, pointing to a woman walking quickly past in the opposite direction. She touches her daughter's hand. "Look! She's got orange cowboy boots on!"

Cosmetics

*T*racy's been jogging lately. She's been jogging with Steve for two months and she feels great. They work together but they don't really know each other. They meet at the elevators twice a week, drive to a path that Steve discovered during a bike ride one weekend with his friend, Joe, lace up their shoes, stretch their legs and arms and start jogging. Tracy's never met this man, Joe, this friend of Steve's, but she's heard all about him and she's beginning to wish he'd go jogging with them.

Tracy and Steve look like they've come straight out of a glossy magazine. They don't really like each other because of that. They like jogging together because they have nothing much to talk about. Without needless chatter they can both concentrate on their bodies, on feeling each muscle extend and release, on listening to their healthy, healthy hearts. When Steve talks he usually discusses his friend, Joe. Tracy doesn't know why but she likes to hear about him, about Joe. When Tracy talks she worries about her mother. Steve usually fades out and listens only to his breathing, or sometimes he thinks about what he will have for dinner.

Tracy has never felt beautiful. Not since she was very little and could still sit on her father's knee. She jogs because she's convinced that her bum is spreading. Steve, on the other hand, has always thought he is beautiful, but he doesn't really care about it. He gels his hair in the morning and uses whitener to polish his teeth. Other than that, he's just one of the guys.

This path that Steve found runs from east to west right behind the houses of the Forest Hill elite. Because they start from the south, Steve and Tracy can choose either direction and then jog to one end and back to the beginning. For some reason, even though they've had a choice all this time, they always go west first and then run back to the beginning. But today Steve has nudged Tracy east instead of west and now they're jogging down a new path she's never been on. Of course it's just an extension of their regular path, but it feels new to her. Tracy has always wondered what was down this way and so she doesn't feel as weird as she thinks she should. She feels like this is some sort of test. Something like, "if you can jog down one path you can jog down them all."

They jog curiously down this new path, not saying anything. They jog past a dog who is meandering through the ditch at the edge of the path. The dog has something in its mouth but they are going too fast to see what it is.

"Did you see that?" Tracy says. She is breathless, gulping the air. But her lipstick is staying and that's what counts.

"What?" Steve never sweats. He never breathes hard. This often bothers her but usually not until later, not until after she's had a shower, curled her hair and picked at a good dinner.

"The dog," she says. She is trying to sound like she has just woken up, like there aren't a million oxygen bubbles popping in her lungs.

"Yeah," he says. Steve is thinking about his tanning appointment tomorrow. He will have to cancel it because he has a lunch meeting.

Maybe he can breathe because he doesn't talk, Tracy thinks, and then her mind goes white blank and she concentrates on catching that second wind. She is convinced that her lungs are in just as great shape as Steve's. She is carrying some extra weight, her breasts, her hair, but her lungs are solid. Tracy lengthens her breathing time and her stride.

They jog on. The houses begin to thin out on each side of the path. They are becoming much larger and the pools and tennis courts begin to take up two lots instead of one. "Look at that." She points towards a mansion they are passing.

There is some sort of garden party going on. The guests are milling about on this huge expanse of lawn in black tuxedos and colourful evening gowns. Tracy and Steve jog past, slowing their pace to take everything in. Steve looks more at the path than at the party. He is imagining himself flanked by beautiful women, standing on the patio with Scotch in a crystal tumbler in his hand. Tracy almost trips over a log while watching a woman in a bright red, sequined gown drink a martini by the pool.

It's getting darker and the path is narrowing ahead.

"Probably political," Steve says. He often regrets advertising. There just isn't enough money in it.

Tracy grunts delicately. She is worrying about the path. They usually jog for twenty minutes one way and then head back. They've only been jogging for sixteen minutes and the path is almost dead.

"The path." Tracy hopes he'll know what she's trying to say because she can't get anything else out of her lungs.

"What?" He doesn't.

"What do we do now?" she forces out and nods her head towards the darkening, thinning path. Her voice is raspy and thick with phlegm. It makes her angry that she even has to say anything. No wonder I don't date him, she thinks. She wipes the sweat off her forehead with the back of her hand and a long pink fingernail catches in her curly hair.

"Keep going," Steve says.

They have to start jogging in single file through the skinny path. Tracy jogs behind him and looks around nervously. Steve looks straight ahead as if nothing is different, as if they are travelling in a luxury coach, west instead of east. She can hear the gradually diminishing sounds of the garden party. Voices and the rustle of leaves begin to mix and the clink of cocktail glasses slowly disappears. Now all Tracy can hear is the blood pounding in her ears and the crunch of gravel below her Nikes. She pulls her black tights down on her thighs and straightens her tank top.

"Back," she says. She has been watching her watch and it just now hit twenty minutes.

"What?"

She feels like tripping him. He breathes smoothly, as if he is walking down the street shopping.

"C'mon. A little further," he says. Steve is getting ahead of her. It's getting darker and Tracy is nervous. She's been brought up to believe that it is only beautiful women who get attacked in dark places, and even though she truly believes she isn't all that beautiful, sometimes she wishes she was hideously ugly, just for the security.

"Let's head back," she says.

"I can't hear you, Tracy," Steve calls out. He doesn't slow down. "What did you say?"

But all of a sudden she sees something moving up ahead, past Steve, past the thorny, creeping bushes.

"Shit." Her mind seizes up on her and the hairs on her neck stand up.

"What?" Steve calls out. He is about ten feet ahead of her and he obviously hasn't seen what's ahead of him. Or if he has, he doesn't care. He is, after all, a tall, strong man with white teeth and beautiful hair.

Up ahead is the shape of a man, walking with a limp towards them. Tracy is getting closer and she can tell that something is terribly wrong with his face. Steve has passed the man, noticing nothing. He keeps jogging.

But she notices. She notices everything. The limping man's face is blue. Blue and red and black, like an accident victim, like he's been burned and peeled and scabbed. Even his neck and his nose and his ears. His mouth and his eyes shine out of this mess, this blue mess of lines and blood-red gore.

"Oh my God," she whispers, or maybe she just thinks it. She feels like she's going to be sick. She can't even imagine what has happened to him, what horrible, disfiguring, disgusting terror he has been through to make him like this. She can't imagine why he doesn't just get plastic surgery. There must be something he can do.

He is wearing a plaid sports coat and baggy cotton pants. The cuffs are coming out everywhere and Tracy notices the pure shabbiness. His hair is greasy blond, tied tightly in a little ponytail, and even the back and sides of his neck are warped by this grotesque blue, lined skin.

"Oh my God." She says it this time and she passes him rapidly and rushes to catch up to Steve.

"Did you see that?" she asks and Steve turns around.

"What?" He is jogging backwards. "What's wrong?"

She is crying uncontrollably for some reason. "God," she gasps. "God, his face." She knows her make-up is running, but, for some reason, she doesn't care.

"What?" Steve jogs on the spot while she stops to control her face, her twitching lips, her watering eyes. "I can't hear you."

"Didn't you see that?" she says.

"What?"

She feels like hitting him. She feels like smacking him right between his perfectly spaced, baby blue eyes; smacking him on his upturned, poised, sickeningly small little nose; pulling out his blond, blond hair; blackening his white, white teeth.

"Don't you look at anything?" she shouts.

"What are you talking about?" Steve stops jogging and looks around him.

"Anything," she shouts and suddenly punches him in the stomach.

"Shit." Steve keels over, but retains his balance. "What the hell is wrong with you, Tracy?"

She works down the hall from him. She only just met him. She doesn't even know him.

"God, I'm sorry, Steve." Tracy sits down on the path carefully. Steve sits down beside her, trying not to land in dirt. "I just . . ." But for some reason she just can't explain it.

They get up after a few minutes and jog back along the path, past the garden party, now lit with lanterns and loud with jazz music. They don't see the man with the blue face but the dog from the ditch passes them carrying a dead squirrel in its mouth. The dog looks proudly up at them. The dog looks as if it thinks it's carrying gold.

"How disgusting," Tracy groans but Steve doesn't say anything.

At work the next day Steve is telling Joe about the jog. Tracy has called in sick and Steve thinks it must be PMS. What else could it be, he asked himself as he drove to work with the windows open and the stereo on to the sports channel.

"So she punched you?" Joe says. He's been wanting to meet this woman, this jogging woman, but he's in a different office and so their paths haven't yet crossed.

"Yeah," Steve says. He is photocopying some papers and Joe is standing by the coffee machine. "Smacked me more like. Not really a punch."

"What for?" Joe says. "You hitting on her?" After Joe says this he feels this weird pang of jealousy. He's never met Tracy but she sure sounds exciting, and even if Steve isn't interested in Tracy, Tracy must be interested in Steve. I mean, look at him, Joe thinks.

"No," Steve says. "I was just jogging and she kept asking me stupid questions and I couldn't hear her."

"Weird." Joe feels weird about all this. He conscientiously rubs his balding spot and then pours himself a coffee and begins to walk out of the photocopy room.

"Oh," Steve calls him back. "I forgot to tell you the strangest thing."

"What?" Joe stops. He turns back to Steve, cradling his coffee mug between his large, thick, hairless fingers.

"There was this guy on the path," Steve says. "It was really freaky at first, I thought he'd been in some sort of accident. His face was blue and there were blobs of red, like blood, around his ears and in certain places on his face."

"Gross." That's all Joe can think of saying.

"Yeah, well, it turns out, as I get closer I look carefully at him and I notice that it's a tattoo."

"What's a tattoo? What are you talking about?"

"His face is covered with a tattoo," Steve says. "Lines and patterns, flowers, all kinds of weird stuff. All over his face and neck and ears. Man, it was freaky, coming at you like that from out of nowhere, on this dark path. I've been thinking about it too. I mean, why would you ever go out and do that to yourself?"

Joe shudders and then shrugs. "Was that after or before she hit you?" He can't get this picture of Tracy smacking Steve out of his head.

"Before," Steve says. "Weird night."

"Yeah, weird." Joe waves to Steve and leaves the photocopy room. He puts his mug on his paper-littered desk and heads to the washroom. As he is entering one of the cubicles he catches a glimpse of his face in the mirror above the sink. He turns and faces himself full on. He imagines covering his entire face in images, in pictures. He imagines how gross that would be, how much it would hurt. But then Joe can't even think about the pain involved—the ears, the nose, pierced with a needle full of ink. A blue face.

Joe moves closer to the mirror and opens his mouth and inspects his cavities. He pulls down his lower lip and looks at his gums. Then Joe closes his mouth and wobbles his cheeks and neck. He has always thought he looks a little like a turkey. He turns away from the mirror and moves into the cubicle.

No wonder she smacked him, Joe thinks. No wonder.

John and
the One-Armed Woman

*J*ohn is at Twigglies Bar watching the sports channel on TV when he first sees the woman with one arm. She is beautiful. She has long, dark hair and sunken eyes. When she smiles at the bartender, a dimple breaks out on her left cheek.

The woman is missing her right arm. John sees the half-stump hanging awkwardly from her shoulder. She is wearing short sleeves, so noticing the missing arm is not all that hard.

Suddenly the woman reaches down beside her stool and pulls up a sleek, bare plastic arm with long, painted fingernails.

John smiles to himself.

The woman places her cigarette in the plastic arm's fingers and then smokes it.

John thinks she must be really drunk. He watches the awkwardness of the stiff plastic arm as it comes towards her face and then moves away. The woman is laughing at herself.

It is eleven-thirty in the morning. Normally John would be at his job at the counter of the Pampered Pets Store. He was there this morning, at nine o'clock—just like every other morning—but Jocelyn had to lay him off. She said that she didn't need the extra help anymore, that everyone was buying scratching posts, food and toys from the huge Pet Valu newly opened down the street. She said all of that but John knows it is because he kicked that poodle yesterday.

What could he have done? The poodle was wrapped erotically around his leg and he had to move to answer the phone. It was the only way to get the poodle off. Who knew the owner was watching? And, if she was watching, why didn't she do something about the poodle in the first place? John sighs.

The woman with the plastic arm looks up at him and smiles.

"Want one?" she asks. She stretches her plastic arm across the bar with a fresh cigarette stuck between the long fingers.

"Sure, thanks." John smiles at her and takes the cigarette from the arm. The woman laughs.

There is hardly anyone in the bar. John, the one-armed woman, the bartender, a waitress, and two guys in painting overalls with dirty hands, drinking beer. The hockey on the sports channel is a repeat of last night's game. John watches anyway.

The woman across from him laughs again. Loudly.

"What's funny?" John asks. He says this with a smile on his face.

The woman doesn't say anything. She holds the plastic arm in the hand of her real arm. She caresses the forearm and then the biceps. She runs her fingers in between the plastic fingers. John notices that the nail polish on her real hand doesn't match the polish on the plastic one.

He looks up at the hockey game. He remembers this play from when he watched it last night, and he remembers it's a good one. The bartender stops rubbing the counter with a rag and also looks appreciatively at the TV set suspended from the ceiling. John smokes the cigarette, sips his beer and cheers with the bartender after the puck hits the post and then bounces in the net. Even though he saw the same game last night John still gets goose bumps on his neck. Whenever he sees something he admires, something great and noble, he gets goose bumps in strange places. Like when he looks at the beautiful one-armed woman he gets goose bumps on his thighs.

She is smiling at him again. She pushes the plastic hand through her hair and it gets stuck. John laughs but only because she is laughing at herself. As she untangles the stiff fingers from her long hair, John sends the bartender over to her with a drink.

She accepts it and then beckons John to her with the plastic arm. When she extends the arm from her real arm, it reaches right across the bar. It almost touches John. He blushes.

"Hi," he says when he is comfortably seated to the right of her. He looks at her face, her bloodshot eyes and then her stump. It is scarred and gangly. John gets goose bumps on his thighs.

"Hi." Her voice is slurred and low. She flutters her eyes at him, pretending to flirt. She's not very good at it. John clears his throat nervously. He is suddenly aware of his smell, his dog-food–cat-food smell. And that faint odour of cat urine on the knees of his jeans.

"Thanks for the drink," she says. She holds up the gin and tonic and clinks it against his beer.

"I didn't know what you were drinking . . ."

"This is fine. Just fine." The woman takes the drink down in one gulp and then lets out a tiny, delicate, soft, dry burp.

John looks up at the TV. There is a curling match on and he pretends he's interested. The bartender cleans glasses behind the bar and occasionally yawns. The painters are talking loudly from the booth. They are discussing politics and job opportunities.

"So, what do you do?" the woman asks. She flips her long hair out of her face and turns to face John. The plastic arm is resting on her crossed legs. She is long and lean, but voluptuous. She has dark brown hair and green eyes. John thinks he may be in love.

"I've just been laid off," John says. He laughs.

She laughs. "Ah," she says. "That's why you're here."

"Yeah, I guess." John smiles at her. He orders more drinks and pulls out his wallet to pay.

"I'll get this round," the woman with one arm says. She nods to the bartender. He writes something down on a pad of paper by the cash register. "Where were you employed?"

"Pampered Pets," John says. "That pet store across the street." John points out the smoky, cloudy windows of the bar at the well-lit pet store directly across from them.

"Oh." The woman doesn't look impressed.

John hears one of the painters say, "Beware of anything that requires a smile and a kindly disposition." The other painter is silent. John looks over at them. They are staring at the table, looking for all the world as if they are praying.

"Get a load of those two," John whispers to the one-armed woman. He is trying to distract her from thinking that he is too much of a loser.

"Who?" The woman turns around on her stool and stares at the painters. Then she laughs out loud. "The one guy looks like Jesus," she says, loudly.

"Shhhh," John whispers. The woman is laughing and staring at the two men. She picks up her plastic arm and points towards the one who looks like Jesus.

"That one," she shouts. "That one looks like Jesus."

The two men look up at her. The Jesus-looking one blushes. His friend laughs.

"Nice arm," the one painter says. John shrinks on his stool. He looks out the window at the Pampered Pets Store and wishes with all his might that this was a bad dream.

"Thank you," the woman says. She says this genuinely. "I think it's just lovely." She caresses it and then places it in her lap again. She turns back to John.

"Sit up," she says. "You're slouching."

John swallows his beer loudly.

"You don't like my arm, do you?"

"Yes, I do."

"Why haven't you mentioned it then?"

"I—"

The woman holds up the arm and John admires it.

"You can hold it if you want to."

John takes the arm from the woman and holds it. He doesn't know what to do with it. He is afraid to place it in his lap. He doesn't want to offend anyone. If he puts it on the counter, that might look disrespectful. John holds the arm out in front of him, carefully, and sighs.

"Beautiful, isn't it?"

"Yes, it is."

"The moulding, the lifelike quality, the long fingers—it's all done so nicely."

"Yes, I guess it is."

The curling on TV is noisy. John tries to ignore the shouts and the heavy breathing and that sweep-sweeping sound. He tries to concentrate on the conversation with the one-armed woman. He holds her plastic arm and thinks about what he should say next.

"I stole it," the woman says.

"What?"

"I stole the arm." The woman laughs. She orders another drink and one for John. She tells the bartender to write them on her tab.

One of the painters, the Jesus look-alike, says, loudly, "Don't worry, Dan, the economy has a way of circling around and moving back to the same position. We're just in a funk right now. A deep, black funk."

John's hearing seems amplified. It's as if he is the Bionic Woman. It's as if he could lift his scruffy hair up over his ear and then, click, click, click, he could hear everything behind closed doors.

The curlers cheer and one woman does a little, happy dance on the ice and then falls. Her teammates laugh.

The bartender coughs.

John swallows some beer and hears it slush down his throat and settle in his gut.

"I stole it from that store down the street, the one with the leather stuff in the windows," the woman says. She laughs. "I just walked in, asked to try on several outfits, and, while the saleswoman was getting my change room ready, I popped the arm off the mannequin and walked out with it." She sips her drink. "It was genius. Pure genius."

"I thought—" John points to the woman's missing arm.

"You thought this was a prosthetic arm? You thought this was mine?" She laughs.

"I did notice the nail polish was different," John says. He is trying to make her think that he has a little something stored in his skull. "But I thought maybe it was broken and you were going to get it fixed."

"What polish?" The woman looks at the nails on the hand of the plastic arm, which John has placed carefully on the counter. "Oh yeah, you're right."

"People expect to suffer economically," the painter says. His friend says "Yep," and then burps.

John thinks of that poodle he kicked, how it was wrapped around his leg so tightly that it actually hurt. He thinks of the far-away, dreamy look in that poodle's eyes.

He feels slightly sick.

"Should I have a prosthetic arm?" The woman's voice comes at him from afar. Her voice sounds suddenly hollow and empty.

John thinks he's had too much to drink but he can't stop himself. The lunch-hour crowd, two men in suits, have come in, and the noise has suddenly become overwhelming. John orders more to drink and gulps loudly.

"Should I?"

He looks at the one-armed woman. She is lovely and sad. Beautiful. She sits delicately on her stool, holding her plastic arm. Her long legs are crossed, and John can see the muscles in her thighs beneath her skirt.

"You are beautiful," John says.

"Oh shit." The woman lights a cigarette and blows the smoke in John's direction.

"What?" John scratches his head.

The curlers wrap up their game and leave the ice with their arms around each other. The sports news comes on. John looks out the window and sees Jocelyn at the Pampered Pets Store helping an old woman load her car with a twenty-pound bag of cat food. Jocelyn's fat body jiggles as she waddles towards the car and throws the bag into the back seat. She wipes her chest off and the lap of her pants. Then she shakes the old woman's hand.

"I said, *Shit!*"

"I heard you."

The woman glares at John. He looks at her and smiles sheepishly.

"I really think you are good-looking," he says. "I think that your arm makes you even better looking."

The woman laughs. "That's a new one."

"A new what?"

"A new pick-up line."

The painters get up from their booth. The Jesus look-alike passes by the one-armed woman and pokes her on the shoulder. "A fine plastic arm you've got there, Miss," he says.

"Why thank you." The one-armed woman holds up the plastic arm and uses it to shake hands with the painter. He laughs and then the painters leave the bar and climb into a van with "Eddie's Painting Miracles" written on the sides.

"I'm not trying to pick you up," John says."I've just lost my job."

"Not much of a job, though," the woman says. She signals with her thumb over to the Pampered Pets Store.

"It was a job." John buries his face in his arms on the counter. That dreamy expression the poodle was making yesterday is really starting to eat at him. He looks down at the leg of his jeans, expecting to see something. There is nothing there. The bartender looks at the one-armed woman and makes a cutting motion with his fingers across his neck. Then he points to John. The woman nods.

"Well, I've lost my arm."

John looks up. He swallows his saliva loudly. He looks at his empty beer glass and then at the bartender who shakes his head back and forth, saying no, saying you're cut off.

"Yes, I guess you have," John whispers.

"That's much worse than losing a job at a pet-food store."

The woman looks down at the plastic arm lying on her legs. "Much, much worse."

"I think you're right." John feels horrible. He feels physically ill and mentally depressed. A huge weight settles on his shoulders. He slouches on his stool.

The one-armed woman moves closer to John. She lifts her stump up and touches him with it. She positions it carefully on his slouched shoulder and begins to move it up and down. He watches this as if it isn't his body she is touching. He looks at her stump, missing everything below the elbow, and he gets goose bumps on his thighs. A warm feeling clouds his body, a warm satisfied feeling, and he smiles.

"Thanks," he says.

"The magic, healing stump." The woman laughs. "I should go now. I've got things to do and people to see."

John smiles at her. "I think a prosthetic arm would look silly on you. Like a bald man wearing a hairpiece."

She laughs. "Good-bye," she says. She passes the bartender and whispers something in his ear. He nods. She takes her purse and her plastic arm and walks towards the door of the bar. She opens the door.

John turns back to the sports channel and watches the highlights from last night's hockey game. The famous shot is scored again and again, and John gets goose bumps on his neck.

"Hey," the bartender says. "Hey, buddy. I've got something for you."

"What?" John looks over at the bartender. In his hand he is holding the plastic arm.

"She wanted you to have this. For good luck," he says. He laughs.

John smiles. He takes the plastic arm from the bartender and holds it in his arms like a baby. And, as he watches the rest of the sports news, he swears he can feel heat coming from the arm. He can feel it twitching and flexing. He feels its warmth and vitality travel right through his animal-scented shirt, straight through to his heart.

An Urban Myth

"They didn't know what was wrong with him," Sara says as she reaches across the table for the sugar bowl. Don looks quickly at her and then looks down into his empty mug. Sara spoons sugar into her cappuccino and then stirs. "He was having headaches and falling over all the time. Needless to say, Becky was having a fit."

Don shivers. He coughs. He touches the corners of his watering eyes with his napkin.

"So, what did she do?" Emily asks. She digs into her slice of pie. She has scooped all the whipping cream off and it is melting in a pile beside the slice. A slight breeze on the warm patio causes Emily to hold on to her hat with one hand. She uses the other hand to manoeuvre the large pie pieces into her painted mouth.

Don's hand shoots up into the air. He looks like he could be directing traffic. He waves frantically at the waitress.

"More coffee," he shouts.

The waitress rushes past. She doesn't notice Don.

"Well, they took him to a nose doctor to see if it had something to do with his sinuses." Sara pauses for effect.

"Yes? And?" Emily is devouring her pie. She is eating so quickly she is making small noises. She looks around the patio to see if anyone is watching.

Don looks worried. "More coffee," he shouts at the waitress. She is ignoring him. "She's ignoring me," he says.

"Just be patient, Don." Emily pats his hand with the side of her fork. A piece of pie crust drops onto Don's hand and he flicks it off, onto the patio floor. Emily's other hand is still resting on her hat. "Put your hand down and be patient."

Sara clears her throat, waiting for her friends' full attention. Emily smiles at her. Don looks away.

"So, the nose doctor pries around in little Tim's nose for awhile and you wouldn't believe what he finds." Sara takes a gulp of her coffee. Emily stops eating and looks at Sara. Don is giving the evil eye to the waitress.

"Well? What?"

"A pea."

"A pea?"

"There was a pea in his nose."

"No!" Emily lets go of her hat so that she can clap both hands over her mouth. "No! A pea? A green pea? That's disgusting!"

"More coffee," Don shouts at the waitress.

"Becky said that they hadn't had peas for dinner in several days. That means the pea had been in there for days." Sara likes telling this story. She likes the effect. She smiles.

"Do you think I should go get the coffee myself?" Don asks.

"Was the pea squished or whole?" Emily asks. She finishes her pie and sits back in her chair. She is holding her hat again and she looks a bit like a resting ballerina.

"I don't know. I didn't ask. But can you imagine?"

Sara and Emily laugh.

"I had a penny up my nose once," Don says quietly.

Sara and Emily look quickly at Don. They look at him as if he has just arrived.

"What?"

"A penny." Don leans back on his chair. He coughs again. He rubs his hands over his face. He hasn't shaved in days and the stubble is driving him crazy. When he first arrived at the cafe Sara said he smelled. She said he smelled like rotten cheese.

"Coffee?" the waitress asks. She fills up Don's huge mug. Don glares at her but she doesn't look at him.

"Tell us!" Sara and Emily say together.

Don takes a large gulp of his black coffee. "I don't know how it happened. I was way too young. All I know is that I had to go to the hospital to get it out."

"That's worse than a pea."

"Way worse!"

Sara and Emily look at Don in a new way. They stare hard at his nose.

"What I want to know is how? I mean, how could you possibly stuff a penny up your nose?"

"I don't know." Don is sipping his coffee quickly. He blows on it and then he sips it and then he blows on it.

"Stop that."

"What?"

"Stop slurping and blowing on your coffee. It sounds disgusting." Emily glares at Don.

"Can I have another cappuccino?" Sara asks the waitress.

The waitress nods energetically at Sara. "Right away," she says.

"So how did they get it out?" Emily asks.

"How did you get her to listen to you?" Don asks.

"Who?"

"The waitress."

Sara shrugs.

"How did they get it out, Don?"

Sara looks at Emily. "Probably with tongs," she says. "Small ones, like tweezers."

"She never pays attention to me. We've been coming here every Sunday in the summer for years and she never refills my coffee cup." Don blows and sips his coffee loudly.

Emily and Sara ignore him.

"That's a funny word, isn't it?" Emily says.

"What is?"

"Tweezers."

Sara laughs. Her cappuccino arrives and she swirls it around in the mug. She licks at the foam and then makes a face. "Ugh, I wanted chocolate, not cinnamon. There's nothing worse than getting cinnamon when you wanted chocolate."

"My mother once told me that her sister swallowed a pin when she was a baby," Emily says.

"That could kill you." Sara looks concerned. She has foam on her upper lip.

"Maybe it was a safety pin," Emily says.

"And maybe it was closed," Don says. He laughs. "Good story, Emily." His laughter quickly turns into a cough. His body is wracked with movement as the cough slowly loosens and then disappears.

"What about the one where the kid climbs out of the pool and bumps his leg on the side?" Emily says. She lets go of her hat and uses her hands to speak. "Didn't he have a lump on his leg and then he hits it on the side of the pool and cracks it and a bunch of baby spiders climb out? Something like that."

"What are you talking about?" Sara looks confused.

"Urban myths," Emily says. "Like the pea and the penny and the safety pin. You know, the alligators in the sewers, the snake in the toilet bowl."

"But I did put a penny up my nose, Emily. It can't be a myth if it really happened to me," Don says.

"True." Emily looks around the patio. She is suddenly bored with the conversation. There is a handsome man sitting alone in the corner pretending to read a book and drinking a caffè latte. Emily smiles at him but he looks past her, out at the street. The breeze picks up and Emily can feel her hat being tugged off her head.

Sara is staring at Don.

"So, what's with the lack of cleanliness, Don?"

"What?" He rubs his hands through his hair.

"Why do you smell so bad? Why haven't you shaved lately? What's going on?"

"He doesn't smell that bad," Emily says. She says it out the corner of her mouth while she tries to catch the attention of the man in the corner of the patio. He looks from her to the street and then back at her again. She fluffs her hair and smiles.

Sara and Don look at her, look at the man and then look at each other. They shrug.

"I've just been busy."

"Too busy to shower? Impossible!" Sara pulls a compact out of her purse and fixes her lipstick. Don looks at the rim of her cappuccino cup.

"Why do you put that stuff on if it just comes off on everything anyway?"

"He's looking at me," Emily whispers. "That gorgeous man is looking at me."

"He's got a wedding ring on," Sara says. She finishes applying her lipstick and smacks her lips together tightly. Don watches.

"I've just been sleeping a lot," Don says. "I'm not really all that busy, it's just that I can't seem to wake up in time to shower. I've just been really tired lately. And I can't get rid of this cough."

"He does not. I can't see any ring." Emily shades her eyes with her hand and stares over at the man. He is shifting uncomfortably in his chair.

"What about the urban myth where the woman flirts with all these married men and then becomes obsessed with them and follows them when they don't leave their wives?" Sara says sarcastically. She regrets saying it as soon as it comes out. "Sorry," she says. "Oh God, I'm sorry."

"What are you talking about, Sara?" Emily says. "What is that supposed to mean? What do you mean by that?" She focuses all her attention on Sara. The wind picks up and her hat comes off. "Shit."

"I set my alarm every morning, I drink coffee all day long, I never seem to have time to shower at night, I work all day, I've never been more tired in all my life. . . ."

"I'll get it." Sara pushes back her chair and races across the patio chasing Emily's hat.

"I can't believe she said that." Emily is still holding on to the top of her head. "Where does she get off saying stuff like that?" She has hat-head and the man in the corner is staring at her. She holds her hair down with both hands. "I never followed him," she says.

"Do you think I should go to the doctor?" Don asks.

"I never followed him anywhere. I didn't care that he went back to her. I just didn't care. Where does she get off—"

"It wouldn't hurt to see my doctor. What's she going to do? Tell me I'm dying?" Don laughs and then looks down into his empty mug.

"What is she doing?" Emily watches as Sara chases the hat up to the man in the corner. He puts out his leg and stops the hat. He smiles at Sara. She bends down and says something to him and then he writes something on a piece of his napkin and hands it to her. She smiles at him and then saunters back to the table.

"I've also got these spots on my arms and my neck. And, if you must know, I've had really bad diarrhea. It's probably the coffee, I know, but it still worries me. . . ."

Sara hands Emily her hat.

"What did he give you? What did he write down?" Emily asks. She plops the hat back on her head.

"Here." Sara passes Emily the napkin. "He is wearing a wedding band, you know."

"So what?" Emily is smiling widely. She holds the piece of napkin in her hand and smiles widely. "Maybe he'll leave her. Maybe they have a bad relationship. Maybe this will be different."

Sara groans. Emily glares at her.

"I think I'll go to the doctor tomorrow," Don says. "I think I'll just walk into her office and tell her what's wrong." Don starts coughing and he just can't stop. He puts his hands up to clear his breathing tract but he is too tired to hold them up for long. They fall to the table with a crash. The coffee mugs and bowls, the pie plate all jump and rumble. The noise makes people's heads turn.

Sara and Emily look at Don. He looks pale and sickly. He stops coughing and pants. Sara takes his hand.

"Are you OK, Don? You don't look so well."

Emily pats his other hand. She pats his hand softly and then suddenly she lets out a little laugh.

"What is it?" Don looks hurt. "What's so funny?"

"Maybe," Emily says as she clutches the little piece of napkin from the man across the patio, "maybe you have a pea up your nose."

The Orange

"*H*ow do you know, Rebecca?" she says.

We are sitting at the picnic table on a Thursday afternoon. Julie just quit her job.

I mean just. She came home half an hour ago unemployed. I've been home all day. I've been unemployed for almost a year.

We are sitting at the picnic table. I am sucking on the skin of the last orange and Julie is looking through the paper for another job. It's summer.

"How do you know?" she repeats. She holds the paper up close to her eyes and squints at the black print. "How could you know?" Julie drops the paper to the ground and stares at me. She looks tired.

I can't think straight. The sun is getting to me. I just woke up, I haven't had my coffee. The sun is hot and we're all out of oranges.

Shit.

I can't believe I told her about it in the first place.

She caught me off guard.

I'm angry about the fact that we are all out of oranges.

"I just do," I say. "I just know, that's all."

The peel I'm sucking on is starting to make me feel sick. It just isn't the same as the fruit. It's bitter. I'm looking around the back yard, swinging my head back and forth, hoping like hell an orange tree will miraculously appear. I'm looking around, ignoring Julie, and I swear to God I'm almost drooling. All I can think about is one more orange.

"How could you know?" she says. "Becky?" She touches my hand to get my attention.

"I just know," I say. "Somebody I ran into told me." I'm watching her hand touch mine. I can feel shivers running up and down my spine. It feels great.

"But that doesn't make any sense," she says. She's almost talking to herself, she's thinking so hard. "It doesn't make sense at all, Rebecca. How would anyone else know? Who knows? Who was it you ran into?"

I need to stretch but I don't want to take my hand away. The boards from the picnic table are poking into my skin. I'm beginning to wish we had varnished the table and seats. I'm getting splinters on the backs of my thighs.

"Look, all I said was that I thought they had split up," I say. "I thought their relationship was over." I am starting to wish I was a mute. I am starting to wish I had been mute several minutes before.

Julie takes her hand off mine. She scratches her head. She has nice golden blond hair and it's practically glowing in the sun.

"You're testing me, aren't you? You think I'll go back out with him if I know that they broke up? That's it, isn't it?" She looks so excited that I almost want to agree.

So I do.

I nod.

But she doesn't believe me.

"You ran into him, didn't you?" she says. "You saw him somewhere."

This startles me. It's almost like she can read my thoughts. We've been house-mates for almost a year now and she's reading my mind. We even get our periods at the same time every month. Sometimes stuff like that just blows me away.

"It's because of smoking," I say.

"What? What are you talking about?" Julie looks bewildered.

"Oranges," I say. "I started eating them when I quit smoking and now I'm addicted to them."

"When did you run into him?" she asks.

I get up from the picnic table and walk over to the compost bin. I hold my orange peel in one hand and I squeeze my nose shut with the thumb and forefinger of my other hand.

"Can you open this for me?" I sound like I have a cold. "I'm all stubbed up," I say. I'm goofing around but Julie doesn't think I'm being so funny. She walks over to the compost bin and opens it for me. I throw the peel in.

"It doesn't even smell," she says. "I never smell it."

I am beginning to think Julie can't smell anything. We have these two cats and their litter can go for weeks without Julie smelling it. I tried that once. I stopped cleaning the litter for a week and Julie didn't notice a thing. The cats sure noticed. They stopped using the litter pan and used my bed. I had to feel sorry for the cats. I guess if I were in their position I would use something else too.

"I can't believe they broke up," Julie says. "He told me they were perfect for each other."

Then there's the matter of food. Everything tastes good to Julie. Everything. And taste has everything to do with smell. I could probably put a rotten egg in front of her and break it. She wouldn't even smell it. She just doesn't notice anything.

"Let's have a beer, OK?" Julie smooths her skirt down and goes into the house. I can hear her talking to the cats.

I think about his break-up and how it's going to impact on my life. I've finally come to terms with all this and now . . . I feel like bashing my head against the compost bin.

"Maybe I just imagined the whole thing," I call out. She can hear me through the open kitchen window. "Maybe I only think I know. Just like you said." I am sounding so stupid now that I do bash my head. Twice. The compost bin is soft plastic so it doesn't really hurt. But the stench is unbearable when my head is that close.

Julie comes out of the house carrying two beers and a bag of potato chips. Salt and vinegar. The ripply kind. I take a beer from her and walk back to the picnic table. I'm still half-looking for oranges in the garden. Julie planted tomatoes and carrots, but no oranges.

"Why didn't you plant an orange tree?" I ask.

She looks at me like I've just now fallen down from the sky. She shakes her head. She's still thinking about him. I can tell.

"I wish we had an umbrella," Julie says. The sun is hot and it's shining right down upon the table. My hair feels like it's on fire. I touch it. Julie's looks cool because it's blond. I try to touch it but for some reason she pulls away.

"Yeah," I say. Maybe she doesn't want to talk about them anymore.

But then she says, "Do you think he still loves me?"

I shrug and swig at my beer. This woman has a one-track mind, I think.

I steal a look at her face. She is looking up into the sky, watching a plane pass overhead. She looks sad, kind of dejected. I can't stop thinking about the time he left her and how I was there for her. How I've always been there for her and how she never notices. Like smell and taste.

I feel like smacking her. Wake up, I feel like shouting. He's no good, I want to yell. He'll do it again, I scream in my mind. He'll leave you for any woman who looks at him.

"Remember what he did to you?" I can't help but say it.

"Shit," she says and looks right at me. "Shit, I wouldn't go back with him if you paid me."

She doesn't convince me.

"Remember the night of the house party?" I don't want her to forget how mean he can be. What a little asshole he really is. Making out with her friend on her bed, leaving his used condom there. Shit. "At least he used a condom," I say, more to myself than to her.

"Just shut up, Rebecca. OK?" Julie is getting mad. She pulls her beer label apart and throws it onto the ground in pieces.

I touch her hand, I rub her arm. I want her to think about us for a minute. I want to let her know how I've begun to feel. I want to tell her that we could be happy together but I know she won't be interested. I know she won't care. But I really want to tell her.

Just then the phone starts to ring. Julie pulls away from me. We can hear it ring through the kitchen window. Four times. Then the answering machine picks it up. Neither of us moves. We can hear my voice saying "Julie and Becky aren't available at the moment . . ." and then the beep.

There is a slight pause and the wind ruffles the neighbour's laundry next door.

Then I start to talk.

I am loud.

I want to talk over his message.

I want to drown him out.

"I saw him on the street, Julie," I say. "I saw him with two other women. One was large and beautiful. The other was small, dark and skinny. I saw him with his arms around both of them at once and they were walking together like a chorus line. This was just last week. When I was getting asparagus for dinner. That's when I bought the last bag of oranges. That's when he told me that they had broken up, that she had moved out on him."

Julie looks up at me and the answering machine beeps twice in the background. A cloud moves in front of the sun.

"I didn't want him to hurt you again," I say.

She looks at me curiously. I can't help but think that her hair is the exact same shade as that large woman's hair. I can't help but think that, although I really love her, sometimes I just hate her. My stomach is churning and I'm sipping my beer and looking at the picnic table. God, sometimes I just hate her so much.

"So that's how you knew," she finally says. "Is that all?"

How does she know there's more? I want to scream. But instead I start talking and I just can't stop.

"And then we walked together to the market," I say. I feel like I have to get it all off my chest. I feel like she should know everything. I mean, here I am, about to get my heart broken, so I feel like breaking hers too.

"Go on."

"He left those two women and went to the market with me." I pause. I can't get it out. It's like it's stuck in my throat.

"What next?" She is looking right into my face. I can feel her stare. It is hot and angry.

"Well, I bought oranges and asparagus."

"Becky!" She smacks me on my upper arm. I look up at her.

"I told him we were together," I say.

"What do you mean? What the hell does that mean?"

"I told him we were lovers," I say. "I told him you were my girlfriend and that he couldn't have you. He laughed, you know. He laughed and said, 'Julie and Rebecca, what a pair!'"

"Holy shit." Julie jumps up from the picnic table, knocking over her beer bottle. We both watch as the beer pours golden out into the sunshine. "My God, Rebecca," she says. "Oh my God."

"I didn't want you to get hurt again," I say but she already knows the real truth. You can tell. I can see her mind moving a mile a minute. A little frown overtakes her face and soon her forehead is all crinkled. She looks a bit like she is going to be sick.

"How could you?" She is screaming. "Why?"

I don't know what to say. I look around at the neighbours' yards. No one is outside yet. It is Thursday afternoon and most people are working.

"I just can't believe it, Rebecca."

You knew, I think. You had to have known.

Julie sits back down. She moves away from me and picks up her empty beer bottle. "I didn't know," she says. "I had no idea."

"Well." I can't think of anything to say.

"How long have you been . . . ? How long has this been . . . ?" Julie's voice trails off. "Don't answer that, OK? I don't want to know." She puts her hand up when I try to say something.

We sit there, silently, in the sun.

She won't look at me after that, and, a little later, she gets up and goes in to listen to the answering machine.

I sit out in the back yard for a couple of hours, watching the sun move across the sky. I keep wishing that I had another orange peel to suck on. I even briefly think of opening up the compost and fetching an old one from out of there.

Later, when it gets dark, I get up from the picnic table and stretch my legs. I go into the house. The message on the answering machine has been erased and Julie is gone. The odour from the compost bin outside wafts through the kitchen window and into the house. It mixes nicely with the smell of well-used cat litter. I open the fridge and look in. I root around for awhile, moving things and cleaning out the crisper bin. I throw out the leftover pasta and a mouldy tomato.

And then, all of a sudden, I see it.

I can't believe it.

There is one last orange in the fridge. There, behind the ketchup bottle.

How could I have missed it?

All this time there was one more orange in the fridge.

Two Hours North
of the City

"*F*ishing is not romantic," she says. "I really don't care what Hemingway says, Darren, fishing just isn't my cup of tea."

She is holding a spinner in her left hand as she says this. She is holding it away from her body, between her thumb and forefinger. She looks as if she is afraid of the spinner. She looks as if she thinks it will bite her.

I nod in her direction. "Give it a chance," I say.

"Humph." She is down by the edge of the rock, tossing her line awkwardly into the current. We are both trying to be civil but she is testing my patience.

I look out into the river. I think of the giant trout I will catch. I think about his liquid silver fins right there in front of me and about how everything will change once I catch him.

"This is boring," she says. I look over at her. She is sitting on the rock, her pole resting in the water, her line dragging through the rapids.

"Pull it up," I say. "Marge, pull it up."

"I'm bored stiff, Darren. At least we could do something fun."

I walk up to Marge's line and pull. It's stuck.

"See," I say.

Marge shades her eyes and looks into the distance.

I cut the line free and follow it up to Marge's pole.

"Darren, honey."

"What?" I am sitting down beside her, staring out into the river. I think I just saw a trout jump. My body is tense and alert. I feel a bit like that Hemingway character, a bit like that kid who's always fishing. The one whose dad is a doctor. Nick, I think. I think his name is Nick, but I'm feeling too lazy to look it up. I also feel like the guy who wrote that book about the brothers and the river. Actually, I feel like the brothers, not the writer. I feel like every fishing guy who has ever felt this way. That's how I feel.

I look at Marge. Her hair is beautiful in the morning sun. Silver blond. It's the same colour as trout. She is lying down on the rock now and her eyes are closed.

"Darren," she says again.

"Hmmm?" From where I'm sitting I reel the lines in and put the poles beside me. I lie down beside her.

"Let's go home, honey," she says.

I don't really want to hear that from her. We are only three days into our vacation.

"No," I say.

Marge leans up on her elbow and glares down at me. She looks at me for awhile. Even though my eyes are closed I can feel her staring. Then she leans back down and falls asleep.

Marge and I are in the midst of planning our vacation. We have the pamphlets spread out all over the kitchen table and we are leafing through them and tossing the ones we don't like over our shoulders. Marge is wearing a turquoise skirt, a black jacket and lipstick. She has just come back from the bank where she is a teller. She was promoted last week and now she can sign her own slips instead of asking the manager to do it.

"What about Brazil?"

"What about Mexico?"

"What about Vancouver?"

Marge has all these fantastic ideas about where we should travel.

"We don't have that kind of money," I say.

"What about one of those package deals in the Caribbean? They're cheap. Or a cruise. We could go on a cruise."

Marge takes off her jacket and adjusts her blouse. I can see her lacy bra through the sheer material of the blouse. Her long, painted nails flick through her hair and I can smell the scent of sunflowers.

I've never been on a holiday with Marge. I used to go fishing with Richard Conner before I married Marge. We've only been married a year and so I didn't think it was fair to leave her behind this time. And besides, Richard is going fishing with Joe Mendley this year and they didn't bother to invite me.

"What about Florida? We could drive down." Marge is beginning to get the picture.

"Florida sounds OK," I say. And then I think about renting a car, the hotel fees and the dinners out. When I say "Maybe we can borrow Bernie's camper," Marge's face falls.

"What about a cottage somewhere?" Marge asks. "Surely we can afford a cottage. You can cook." She giggles.

I don't see what's so funny about that. Marge hands me a pamphlet entitled "Cottages of the North." I leaf through it quickly. Nothing much appeals to me until I see a little box of writing on the back panel right at the bottom. I hold it up to my face. It reads:

Small fishing cottage for rent between July and August. $100 per week. Secluded. River front property. Bring own poles. 676-0094 ask for Bob.

I read the ad twice just to make sure and then I carefully show it to Marge. She takes the pamphlet in her long fingers, between her bright pink nails. She holds it like it has fleas.

"Oh God," she says. "River-front property. I could work on my tan."

Somehow the fishing part has gone right over her head. I smile.

"Let's do it," I say.

"I wonder if there's a fireplace." Marge has this thing for fireplaces. I think if we had a fireplace Marge would move everything into the living room and just sit in front of the fire for the rest of her life.

"Ask if it has a fireplace," she says loudly as I dial the number. At first I get an operator who tells me to dial the area code. She says it's a long-distance call. So I dial the area code and the number and the phone rings and rings and rings. I think about a little old couple living in a cottage out by a large roaring river. I think of the old man named Bob hobbling to the phone, anxious to get back to his Scrabble game with his wife. Their fire cracks loudly in the distance. The smell of cherry pie wafts through the cottage.

"Bond Hotel," a voice on the other end of the phone says.

"I'm . . . uh." I can't think of what to say. Marge is standing beside me, real close, and her perfume is hanging in the air. "Ask about the fireplace," she whispers. "Don't forget."

"I'm calling about an ad," I say. "For a cottage."

I hear the phone crash down and then a voice screams "Bob" into the distance. I can hear a band playing, or maybe it's just a jukebox. I hear glasses clinking and people talking loudly.

"What do you want?" The voice is gruff.

"I'm calling about your cottage," I say into the phone.

"You want it?" the voice barks. I figure this is Bob.

"Could you tell me a little about it?"

"What do you want to know?" Bob asks. He sounds slightly drunk. He slurs his words together that way. Like he's drunk.

I hesitate but Marge is poking me.

"Does it have a fireplace?" I ask.

"What do you need a fireplace in the summer for?" Bob asks. He's got me there. I pretend that he has said something satisfactory. I nod to Marge.

"Is there good fishing?" I ask.

Marge is clapping her hands softly and singing "A fireplace, a fireplace."

"Look, Mister. You want the cottage or not?" Bob says.

I take a chance. "Yes," I say. "We'll take it for the last two weeks of July."

When I get off the phone Marge starts pestering me.

"What did he say? What's it like?"

For some reason, I don't know why, I tell her all about the cottage. I tell her about the cathedral ceiling in the living room and the open-concept dining/kitchen area. I tell her the walls are all pine wood and the stove is brand new. I tell her that Bob says we will be lulled to sleep by the sound of the river outside the bedroom window. Marge's face glows. I tell her all about the fireplace—large grey stones, not brick.

When Marge wakes up by the river she has a sunburn on her face.

"Shit, Darren," she says. "Why didn't you wake me?"

I'm fishing a little upstream from where she was sleeping and I choose to ignore the question.

"What time is it?" she calls.

"Eleven-thirty," I say.

"When are you going to be finished?"

Marge doesn't understand fishing. You are never finished fishing. Hemingway is fishing in heaven.

"Can we go back and get lunch?" she asks.

"Go ahead," I say. "I'll be back later."

"There is no way in hell I'm going back to that cottage alone, Darren."

We look at each other. Marge is standing up by where she was sleeping and her face is bright red. She smooths her shorts down and adjusts her T-shirt. My fishing hat shades my eyes but for some reason I know she can see right into me.

"Just wait awhile," I call. "Just wait one god-damned minute."

Marge looks like she is going to cry. She has bitten off all her nail polish, pulled and chewed it off in strips. Her eyes are puffy from her nap and her hair is sticking up away from her head, angling out towards the river. She looks away from me.

She squats on the rock, takes off her sandals, and pulls at the nail polish on her toenails. I can hear her talking to herself. Mumbling. It sounds like the river, her mumbling, only a little angrier.

We have loaded up the rental car with three suitcases. Two for Marge. I put my tackle box in the trunk while Marge is closing all the blinds in our apartment. I take apart two poles and carefully place them alongside the tackle box. I've got an anthology of short stories by Hemingway and a guide for identifying fish. Marge has her fashion magazine and her bird book. We set off, surprisingly organized. It is early morning and it seems like no one is awake yet. The streets are clean and the humidity has not yet reached an uncomfortable level.

When we are an hour outside the city we stop for breakfast. I pull the car up beside a red pick-up truck in front of a Dunk-Your-Donuts place. Marge hops out excitedly and slams the car door. I get out and stretch.

"What kind do you want?" she asks. "Cinnamon cruller? Danish? Honey? Chocolate?"

For some reason I am craving a buckwheat cake even though I've never had one before. Buckwheat cakes fried in fat over an open fire sound like just the thing this donut shop should sell.

We walk into the store side by side. I'm feeling jumpy. I'm itching to get at those fish.

"Two cherry Danishes," Marge says to the young girl behind the counter. "And two coffees," she adds.

We take a booth beside the window overlooking the rental car.

"God, this'll be fun," Marge says. "I can't wait to see the cottage."

"Two tranquil weeks of harmony with nature," I say and Marge looks quickly at me.

"Why are you talking like that?" she asks. She smiles nervously.

"It just seemed like something to say," I say.

Our coffee and Danishes arrive. We are hungry and so we eat in silence.

I've taken out my Hemingway book. I keep it in the back pocket of my shorts. I read his description of the Big Two-Hearted river: "The river was clear and smoothly fast in the early morning." I read it over and over again. God, I think. God. I have to put my fishing pole down for this.

Marge has stopped picking her nail polish off her toes and is trying another approach. She has sidled up behind me and has wrapped her pink spotted nails around my stomach. She is rubbing her hips against me, playing with my shorts and whispering things to my neck. The hair on my neck stands up but the rest of me chooses to ignore her.

"Let's go home, honey," she whispers. She licks my neck.

"No, Marge," I say and I can feel her face fall. "Let's just go back for lunch. We'll try a new spot in the afternoon." I put the book back in my pocket and pick up my pole and the bucket of water. I start walking away from her towards the road that leads to the cottage.

Marge picks up the tackle box, her fishing pole, her sunglasses, and follows me. She walks hesitantly, using tiny little steps. Her face is all balled up and she looks like she is going to cry again.

I'm feeling angry. It's not entirely my fault. I want to tell her that everything is not entirely my fault. We walk back to the cottage like this. Marge four paces behind me, my shoulders tense and stiff. Marge is on the verge of tears. Shit, I think. Some vacation.

After we eat our donuts in silence we get back into the car and drive the rest of the way to the cottage. The radio cans out on us about one hour outside the city and we sit quietly for the rest of the way. I've got my window open and I can smell the fresh scent of manure and hay and country air. I breathe deeply. Every once in awhile Marge takes my stickshift hand in hers and traces the veins with her long, pink fingernails.

"Did you remember the key?" she asks after we've turned off the main highway and are sailing down the potholed road towards the cottage.

Bob sent us the key with the receipt of our payment several weeks ago. His note said, "Enjoy Bob." That was it. Enjoy Bob. No comma or anything. Marge had laughed at that. She had said, "I hope he isn't going to be there to enjoy."

I nod my head to Marge. I pat my breast pocket where the key is riding safely.

"Oh, this is exciting," Marge says and checks her lipstick in the mirror on the back of the sun-blind.

"Which way, Marge?" She has the map.

"Left and then right," Marge says without looking at the road.

For some reason the car is moving away from a river and more into the forest. For some reason we went over a bridge and past the river several minutes ago. Marge doesn't notice.

After awhile we turn into the driveway, if you can call it that, and sit in the car staring at the cottage. It takes several minutes for Marge to do anything. I'm waiting for it and I'm feeling very nervous. Then it happens. Marge starts bawling right then and there. She throws her arms up like a movie star and starts to sob and wail. Even though we've been married a year I don't know what to do.

"Shit, Marge," I say when her crying gets louder. It's all I can think of saying.

I get out of the car and walk up to the cottage. I pull the door off its rusty hinges and step into the gloom. All I can hear is Marge howling in the car and the crash of the river sounding far off in the distance.

We get back to the cottage in just under an hour. We are just in time to see a raccoon coming out of the broken window. I can feel Marge shuddering behind me. I am sweating from the long walk. I am thirsty and tired.

"I can't deal with this anymore, Darren," Marge says, quietly.

I don't say anything because we've been over all of this every second for the last couple of days. I put my fishing pole and the bucket of water for washing and drinking on the front step.

Lately I've been thinking a lot about old Ernest, old Papa Hemingway. I've been wondering about what he would have done in our situation. I've been wondering if he would have gone home, back to the city, or if he would have stayed here in this incredible disaster with this pitiful, whining wife. I'm starting to believe that Hemingway would probably have brought more alcohol. And cigarettes. Hemingway would have smoked and drunk, sitting out in the front on the broken lawn chairs in the pile of dirt.

Hemingway's girl would never have chipped all her nail polish off. She wouldn't have accused him of everything, and, if she actually had needed to place the blame on him, she would have said it in symbols, in code, in dry, cynical utterances. She wouldn't have out and out said, "It's your fault, you dope," and she most certainly would never have threatened to leave him. Hemingway's woman would have just shot him in the back, or have boarded another train, or have had an affair with another hunter, or have calmly watched him die in the war, or in the African forest, gnawed by a mean-looking tiger.

"I just can't take this anymore, Darren," Marge says again, and this time I turn around just in time to see her lock both of the car doors and roll up the window on the driver's side. I check my pockets for the keys and then it occurs to me that that was what Marge was doing with my shorts on the rock by the river.

As I watch Marge drive off in a cloud of dust and spraying rocks I think about how great she really is. I think about how, if Marge were a Hemingway character, I'd be stuck here, abandoned. I think about how if I were in a Hemingway story I would be holding some huge trout in my hand right about now and Marge would be gone forever.

I think about that all night and right into the next day. I guess I'll be thinking about that for awhile as I sit on the cracked lawn chair in the pile of dirt in front of the broken-down cottage just two hours north of the city.